The Lord Mayor of Death

Marian Babson

Walker and Company
New York

First published in the United States of America
in 1979 by the Walker Publishing Company, Inc.

ISBN: 0-8027-5415-5   R00629 60541

Library of Congress Catalog Card Number: 79-65165

Printed in the United States of America

10 9 8 7 6 5 4 3 2 1

CHAPTER I

The policeman on duty at the desk heard sobbing long before the woman came into sight. He was able to follow her progress down the corridor by the increasing audibility of the sobs. He knew, with the sad resignation of a man long accustomed to the blows of a malicious fate, that she was heading straight for him. And he was alone on duty right now.

Saturday was always a bad day in this district – although not usually so early in the day – and his usual morale raiser didn't always help. He had spent long hours working out and reworking the sums. But there were too many years to go until he reached retirement – decades, in fact.

He fell back on his secondary source of inner strength: how much longer could it be until his transfer finally came through? This district would be the death of him.

The sobs were closer, zeroing in on him. Another domestic quarrel. Another stupid female who'd been knocked around all night and now was coming to the police in the morning.

She'd tell her story, she'd swear out her complaint – fine. They'd got that far before. Then came the hesitations, the second thoughts, the weaseling out – at best. At worst, they both turned on you and let fly. (How dare you interfere between a man and his woman? No matter that the woman had invited – insisted on – your interference.) You were in the middle – with both hands raised against you. Who'd be a policeman? Who'd try to uphold law and justice in the middle of a domestic dispute?

How long was it likely to be before his transfer came through?

She was in the doorway now, her face partially hidden by the paper handkerchief she was using. Even as he watched, she discarded the paper hand-kerchief as an autumn tree discards the faded useless leaves, and produced a fresh one from some recess of her handbag. Almost immediately it was as damp and limp as the one she had discarded.

She bore no visible marks or bruises, he noted with relief. If the man concerned – husband, lover and/or pimp – had had the circumspection not to leave overt traces, it might be possible to jolly her out of her determination to make him pay for whatever it was he *had* done. If she could be dissuaded from stripping off – either physically or mentally – to reveal her wounds, it might be possible to keep a clean charge sheet and send her on her way with a word of comfort, if not wisdom, and a cup of tea.

Optimistic to the last, he kept his eyes down-cast, studying a piece of paper on the desk as he heard her cross the room, shuffling and sniffling, to stand before him. If he were to seem sufficiently distant and forbidding there was always an outside chance that she would go away.

'Oh, please – ' she choked. 'Please, you've got to help me!' He looked up into the depths of her pale swimming blue eyes and knew himself to be trapped.

'Yes, madam.' He drew a block of paper to him. 'What can I do for you?'

'It's my Kitty,' she wailed. 'My little Kitty – she's gone!'

'Dear, dear madam – ' He relaxed, becoming almost genial, foreseeing a problem he could eventually foist on to someone at the RSPCA. 'When did you discover your loss?'

'When I got home from the hotel. I work as a chambermaid at the Royal Tudor – '

He nodded. It was one of the newest and biggest of the tourist traps. It advertised itself as being in the middle price range – which was a laugh to anyone not on an American or Japanese package tour. With well over a thousand rooms, it paid well and kept its staff constantly working and usually on overtime. Ex-staff had been known to compare the working conditions unfavourably with a stretch in a Siberian salt mine.

'Now, shall we start at the beginning, madam?' He smiled at her. 'Routine, you know.' Routine was always soothing, it gave people something to cling to in the midst of disruption. 'Your name, please?'

'O'Fahey. Maureen O'Fahey.' She sniffed and dabbed at the tip of her nose, watching him write it down. He saw that, given the right circumstances, she could be quite pretty.

'And – ' he projected as much of the majesty of the law and reassurance as he could muster – 'you've lost your little kitty and want us to find her for you.'

'Oh, God! Oh, God!' She crumpled suddenly, reverting to the noisy sobs which shook her entire body with an agony out of all proportion to her loss. 'Oh, Kitty! My little Kitty!'

'Here – ' He was shaken. He reached out and unlatched the gate, swinging it open to allow her access behind the formal desk counter. 'Come back here and sit down. Would you like a cup of tea?'

Mutely, she shook her head, allowing him to guide her behind the counter and into a chair.

'Now, don't you worry. We'll find her for you,' he said, knowing it was a lie. Find one lone cat, out of the entire feline population of Greater London? 'Now, then – ' Abstractedly, he began doodling a pointed triangular cat face on the pad. 'How long has your little kitty been missing?'

'She was gone when I got home – ' Maureen O'Fahey raised tragic eyes to his. 'About half an hour ago.'

'That isn't so very long now, is it?' He added pointed ears to counterbalance the pointed chin. 'Don't you think you might give her a bit more time to come back on her own?'

'But she *knows* she oughtn't to go off without me –'

'Ah, well.' He sketched in slanting mischievous eyes. 'They don't always understand these things, do they, madam?' As she seemed about to protest the intelligence of her pet, he added quickly, 'Can you give me any description of her? Perhaps a photograph – ?'

'I didn't think to bring one – ' Sobs caught at her voice, tore at her throat again. 'It's old, anyway, and – and they change so fast at that age. She's five years old – and small for her age. But she's got blue-green eyes – more green than blue, really, and lovely red hair. Not a dark red, but that soft coppery red-gold – '

'Green eyes,' he noted down. 'Ginger fur.'

'They – ' Her voice rode up and down on a ground swell of sobs. 'They were going to be taking her school picture any time now, but they haven't done it yet or you could have had that.'

'School?' In the act of adding whiskers to the pointed feline face, he snapped to attention. The room seemed to have grown cold suddenly.

'It's her first year, and she's been enjoying it so much. And it's made it easier for me, knowing she's safe and taken care of all day while I'm out working. And now – And now – ' The tears flooded again.

'Steady now. Just a minute.' He crumpled the top sheet of the pad and pitched it into the waste-basket. 'Let's start again from the beginning. This is your daughter we're talking about?'

'Yes. My Kitty. My little Kitty – '

'All right now.' He began filling in the sheet with a new sense of purpose, and a nagging awareness of time lost. 'Take it easy now. We'll find her for you, Mrs O'Fahey.'

'It's – ' She raised her head, drenched eyes glinting defiance at him even as the bright red tide of colour swamped her face. 'It's *Miss* O'Fahey.'

'All right.' One more complication, but not one he had to worry about. He noted it down.

'She's five years old and she's been missing for . . . how long?' Automatically, he checked his watch against the clock on the wall. Both said ten minutes to eleven.

'I'm not sure. She was gone when I got home, but I stopped along the way – not more than half an hour – to do some shopping. The landlady keeps an eye on her for me weekends once she wakes up, but she hadn't seen her at all this morning, except the back of her – '

'Yes – ' He made rapid notes. There were too many 'she's' and 'hers', but he thought he was sorting it out fairly well until Maureen O'Fahey brought him up sharply once more.

'The back of her – going off down the street with *him* from the building site.'

'What?'

'Oh, she knows she's not to speak to strangers – I've always drilled that into her. But I suppose, us living in the same house and all, and her seeing me talking to him sometimes, she thought it was all right. He wasn't a stranger. How do you explain to a child – ?' Her face was shadowed, haunted by the moments when she might have been able to say something, moments gone by. 'How do you explain that grown-ups talk to people they aren't always friendly with? People they don't even like, sometimes? Isn't there enough devilment waiting for them in this two-faced world without robbing them of their innocence any sooner than you have to?'

'Can you give me his name?' He spoke softly, trying to keep it natural, conversational, lest he jar her off this emotional plateau she seemed to have reached and was balanced so precariously on, above tears, beyond hysteria. 'This man she went off with?'

'Michael Carney – God rot his soul! If he's got one!' Fire flashed from the blue eyes. 'And she didn't – like you say – "go off" with him. Not like that.' Tears quenched the fire and the choking sobs were back, pushing her off the plateau and into incoherence.

'The landlady . . . she saw her . . . carrying one of
. . . of those little red lunch boxes. You know, the
ones all the kids are crazy about right now. Kitty
was that keen to have one – and I was going to get
her one next payday. But she was carrying one
today. *He* must have given it to her. Don't you see?
She was – She was – *lured* away!'

'We'll find her.' He picked up the telephone and
dialled an extension. He spoke briefly and rapidly,
replacing the receiver with the comforting knowledge that reinforcements were on the way. 'Don't
worry. We'll find her.'

'In time?'

That was the question he couldn't answer and
the apology in his eyes set her off again.

'Oh, God! She's so little, so tiny. She doesn't
know what it's all about. She'll never – '

He used the phone again, this time relaying the
name Michael Carney to be checked in Records
for any previous form, ordering tea, and urgently
requesting the presence of a woman police constable
who could stand by Maureen O'Fahey while
further questioning went on. He'd have done that
a long time ago if he hadn't been sidetracked into
thinking it was a lost cat she was on about.

'How do you teach them?' She looked up at him
again. 'How do you explain to a child that there
are people like that in the world? How do you pro-
tect them from the – the *animals* that – ' She bent
double, hiding her face in her hands.

He looked down helplessly, not even trying to
answer. She must know as well as he that the questions were unanswerable. He only hoped that the

woman police constable would hurry – but she wouldn't have any answers either.

Brisk footsteps sounded along the corridor and he moved to greet the newcomer and give him a quiet briefing before he spoke to the woman.

But it wasn't quiet enough. Abruptly, Maureen O'Fahey had stopped sobbing and words resounded across the room in the sudden silence.

'Little girl . . . abducted . . . lodger . . .' The words seemed to reverberate and it was pointless to try to keep them secret. After all, she knew – it was she who had told them.

'I understand, madam – ' the newcomer took the bull by the horns, moving towards her – 'that you have reason to believe that your little girl has been abducted by a child molester – '

'Oh, God! Oh, God! You don't understand at all!' She doubled over in her agony again, her voice drifted up to them, shrill, as it was overtaken by tears.

'Oh, God – it's *worse* than that!'

CHAPTER II

Her legs were aching by the time they reached the top of the stairs. Although Uncle Mike kept hold of her hand, he hadn't looked down at her in a long time. He hadn't spoken either. He was looking straight ahead and she wondered if he had forgotten about her.

At the top, he handed their two tickets to the guard and hurried out on to the pavement. He was almost running. It was too much!

Kitty put both feet together and leaned backwards against his forward impetus, turning herself into a small dragging anchor. He was thus forcibly reminded of her presence, forced to look down at her.

'Uncle Mike,' she said. 'I can't walk that fast.'

He bit down on the impulse to give her a good crack across the face. There were too many witnesses about. He forced himself to smile.

'Sorry,' he said. 'I'll slow down. But – you want to see the parade, don't you?'

'Oh, yes, Uncle Mike.' She loosened up and took several running steps, pulling at his hand. 'Hurry, Uncle Mike!'

He frowned, looking around them. The street was filled with people, most of them adults with one or more children in tow. Probably some of them *were* aunts or uncles, or even cousins, but it made him uneasy, the way she kept shouting out 'Uncle Mike'. They didn't want to attract attention, they must not seem different in any way from those surrounding them.

'Look – ' He halted, pulling her to a standstill. 'Why don't you stop calling me Uncle Mike? Sure, it's an awful mouthful for a little girl like you. Why don't you call me "Da"?'

'Uncle Da?' She looked up at him, wrinkling her forehead at this fresh evidence of the complexity of grown-ups.

'No – not Uncle Da. Just Da. That sounds all right, doesn't it?'

'Ye-es.' She was dubious. 'But why can't I just call you Mike?'

'Never mind why!' He looked around to see if anyone was observing them, had overheard them. But everyone was pushing past, too absorbed in the demands their own brats were making to worry about anyone else's. 'Da is good enough, isn't it?'

'Ye-es, but – '

'Yes, Da,' he corrected sternly.

'Yes, Da,' she echoed obediently, her attention focusing ahead on more important matters. There were Shire horses at the end of the street. Two great dappled greys, red ribbons plaited into their manes and tails, stood waiting for the signal to move forward pulling a brightly painted wagon filled with boys and girls in some kind of costume.

From somewhere in the distance, carried on a soft damp wind, there came the enticing sound of band instruments being warmed up.

'Hurry, Uncle – Hurry, Da!' She tugged at his hand. He had slowed to a pace suitable only for baby steps. 'I can walk faster than *that*!'

He let her set the pace, an erratic one as her

attention was captured by one spectacle after another. But, in that, they were no different from the
other parties of parents and children pouring
towards the Guildhall, the starting point of the
parade.

'Look, Unc – Look, Da – ' She pointed ahead, her
little red lunch box swinging from her hand. 'Look
at the lady dressed up like a black cat!'

'Yes, that's right.' He winced as she swung her
arm down, but it was better not to comment, not
to make her too aware of the toy lunch box. She'd
already remarked on how heavy it was, fortunately
she seemed to have forgotten that now – or she'd
grown used to the weight. 'You'll see a lot of them
in the Show – ' He drew on the knowledge he had
gathered from the newspapers of the past few days.
'They're lucky, see. They're going to be giving
out paper black cats to kids along the way. If you
get one, you can turn it in at the supermarket for
twenty-five-pence-worth of anything you fancy.'

'Will *I* get one?' She seized on the immediate
point.

'You might.' Much good it would do her. 'You
never can tell.'

The answer seemed to satisfy her. At that age,
they couldn't begin to imagine they weren't the
centre of the universe; she was probably already
planning how to spend the token she had no doubt
she would get.

'Look, Da – ' She pointed upwards again, red
lunch box swinging. 'Look at all those people on
the rooftops. What are they doing up there?'

'They're going to watch the parade from up
there,' he said. 'They'll get a better view. But – ' he

added craftily, as a shadow settled over her face –
'they won't get any black cat tokens. The cat
ladies won't go up there. You have to be down
here to get one.'

'*I* might get one.' Her face cleared. 'I *will*.
Won't I, Da?'

'That's right.' He noted with relief how happily
and naturally she had settled down to calling him
'Da'. Of course, the name meant nothing to her,
it was just a word. Not having any Dad of her own,
she had nothing to connect it with. But it projected
reassurance to everyone within hearing distance. He
was just another fond father who had turned out
early on a damp Saturday morning to give his
little girl a treat. Just like the rest of them.

'This was a *good* idea, Da.' She gave a little skip,
and then another, jouncing the little red lunch box
perilously. 'I'm *glad* I came.'

'Don't jump around!' Unexpected fear harshened
his voice. He wasn't afraid to die. But to die like
this, because of the skittishness of an undisciplined
child – 'You're not a monkey – don't jump around
like one!'

'I want to go home.' Instantly, she reacted to the
animosity in his voice, tugging at the hand imprison-
ing hers, trying to free herself. 'I don't like you. I
want my mother!'

'Ah, Kitty – ' Immediately, he was placating,
tightening his grip so as not to lose her. 'Kitty,
don't be cross with me. I'm sorry.' The need to
soothe her, to conciliate, tightened his throat,
narrowed his eyes. (By God, she'd pay for this!)
'I'm clumsy, that's all. I'm not used to children,
you know.' Humbly, 'You'll have to teach me.'

'All right.' She gave another skip as his stomach muscles constricted in protest. The final one, as it turned out, because then she settled down to walk as sedately as a dowager on her way to a royal funeral.

'You have to buy me a flag – ' She slanted a cautious upwards glance at him, to see how he would react to this. 'All the other kids have flags.'

'So they have.' It might be a try-on, but she was right. The bloody Union Jacks were fluttering everywhere. Every brat seemed to have one. 'Next man we see selling them, we'll get you one.'

'Promise?' She gave another skip and his heart lurched.

'It's a promise – if you'll stop jumping around like a monkey.'

'I'm not!' She was indignant. 'I was only skipping, I wasn't jumping! A monkey jumps – ' she crouched, preparatory to demonstrating – 'like this!'

He caught her as she hurtled upwards, absorbing the full force of the jar with his own body. He held her suspended in mid-air a moment.

'Why are your eyes closed, Da?' She looked down on his face in surprise. 'And your face is all wet. Are you hot?'

'That's right.' He lowered her gently to the pavement. 'It's a warm day.' He dried the palms of his hands on the front of his jacket before taking her hand again. 'Too hot to be putting up with any more of your nonsense. If you can't behave yourself, we'll have to go home.'

'No!' The threat subdued her instantly. 'No, Da, I'll be good.' Her eyes brimmed with self-righteous tears. 'I wasn't *doing* anything.'

'You want to settle down and walk like a little lady. Look at all those others – ' He gestured around them at the nearby children. 'Look how nice and polite they're walking. *They* want to see the parade.'

'So do I! So do I!' She tugged impatiently at his hand. 'Come on, Da. We'll be late if you don't hurry. It will be starting.'

He'd come up here because this was where it all began. The floats, the bands, the carriages, the marchers were all waiting patiently in the side streets, ready to feed out and slot into their place in the procession as the whistles blew and the signals were relayed. Once they all left here, they started on their long march and could be picked up again at any point along the route. He wouldn't let her know that, though. Too much knowledge might undermine the faint authority he had gained over her.

'We'll go down this way,' he said. 'It's a short cut.'

'No!' She tugged in the opposite direction. 'Look over there. They've got real live goats over there. I want to see the goats!'

'We don't have time.' He pulled at her hand, but she fought him.

'Only a little minute. It won't take long. I've never seen real live goats before.'

'Better give in, mate – only way to keep the peace!'

'What – ?' He looked up in horror to meet a matey grin from a Cockney with a small boy tugging at either hand, who towed him past in the crowd.

'The only way . . .' The man echoed in mock-despair as they disappeared into the thickening hordes.

Mike Carney stared after him with a cold prickling uneasiness. He'd never expected anyone to even notice him, far less speak to him. That was why he had appropriated Kitty – for a cover. For the first time, it occurred to him that there were unforeseen hazards in this assumed parenthood. It meant that other parents felt they had a right to exchange small talk and jokes with him – especially on an occasion like this. His cover was *too* good – it threatened to admit him to a society he had no wish to join. Essentially a loner, the thought frightened him more than the thought of his mission had ever done.

'Come on!' He jerked at Kitty's hand, nearly tumbling her off her feet as he forced her in the direction he intended to go.

He felt her resistance, saw her mouth open to howl, glanced around desperately to see how many were likely to notice – and had his first stroke of luck.

'Look this way, see – ' he said quickly. 'Those are clowns down there. Real clowns, like on television. You haven't seen any real live clowns before, have you?'

'No.' Miraculously, her mouth shut and her eyes brightened. 'Can we go see *them*?'

'Sure we can. Aren't I just taking you that way?' She was with him now, eager, no longer resisting. 'They're going to have Clover the Clown himself there. Maybe we'll see him right now – before the parade starts. Wouldn't that be great?'

'Oooh, yes, Da. Hurry.' She was now as anxious

to go in his direction as she had been eager to go
in the opposite direction earlier. She seemed about
to skip again but, with a sudden anxious upward
glance at him, she resisted the temptation and
proceeded at a rapid, but steady, pace.

'Good girl.' He began to relax. It wasn't so hard,
after all. Kids did what you told them – one way or
another. It was better to coax them into doing
what you wanted than to hit them – the trouble was,
it took longer.

He glanced down at her complacently – and his
blood froze. 'Stop that!' he shouted. 'Stop doing
that!'

'What?' She looked up at him in consternation.
He was being a mysterious, unreasonable grown-
up again – angry at her for no reason at all. 'I wasn't
doing *anything*.'

'Stop swinging your new lunch box like that!'
He swept the back of his free hand across his suddenly
dripping forehead and watched her register afresh
the strange incomprehensibility of adults. He realized
that it had been a mistake to draw her attention
to it. She had nearly forgotten she had it, forgotten
the novelty of it – now she was reminded. And dis-
satisfied.

'Why?' She swung it deliberately, unaware of
the effort it cost him not to crack the back of his
hand across her smug little face.

'Because I say so!' (Oh, God, just let him get
her for one moment in a place where there weren't
five hundred witnesses milling about!) 'And I gave
it to you, didn't I?'

'Ye-es.' She admitted it reluctantly. 'But it's
mine now, so why can't I do what I want with it?'

'Because I say so.' It was inadequate, but it was the answer his mother had given him most of the time. With that crack across the face the only authority she had – or needed – to back it up. It had always silenced him, but today's brats were spoiled rotten, recognizing no authority, bowing to no one's rule. (Not without that crack across the face – and there were still too many witnesses.)

'If I don't swing it – ' she was crafty, bargaining – 'then can I open it?'

'Not yet.' He forced himself to smile. 'I've told you. It's a surprise.'

'A surprise for *me*?'

'For you – and for a lot of other people.' His mouth curved grimly.

'For *me*.' Her own mouth curved in unambiguous delight. 'And – and *everybody*.' The smile wavered and dipped. 'Then why can't I open it now?'

'Because it's still too soon.' He watched her begin to react the way she ought, falling in line with his plan. 'You don't want to spoil the surprise, do you?'

'Oh, no, Da.' She was earnest, assuring. 'I'll wait until you tell me I can.' Then a sudden qualm seized her. 'You'll tell me when I can, won't you?'

'Oh, you needn't worry,' he assured her. 'I'll tell you. And then everybody will have a great big surprise they'll remember to the end of their days.'

CHAPTER III

Sir Guy Carraway raised his head as Elaine, Lady Carraway, adjusted the glittering chain of office over his dark robes. The plumed hat waited to be donned, only to be doffed again and again to the cheering multitudes who would be lining the route of the procession.

'Will I do?' he asked, having already read the answer in her proud eyes.

'You'll do,' she said.

Lucky Guy. Everyone called him that. Lucky Sir Guy Carraway, Lord Mayor of London. At moments like this, he believed it himself.

'I *am* a lucky guy,' he said.

'You always were.' She gave the chain a final pat for good luck, laughing softly.

Lucky Guy. They had called him that since the Korean War when he had led a mixed platoon of assorted nationalities across a minefield – without even knowing it was there. The remnants of other officers' defeats, the men had followed him because they had believed he knew what he was doing. He hadn't, but he hadn't needed to. He had had luck instead of knowledge. And that was what counted. Not just having luck, but having the kind of luck that could rub off on everyone around you, draw them into the magic circle of your own luck. That was when they rushed to cluster around you, trusting to your luck as they could never trust to their own. That was when the legend formed and began to grow. The legend that brought more and more people from all walks of life to come and try to crowd into your shadow, hoping that your luck might touch them, transform their lives as it had transformed your own.

Lucky Guy.

'A Guy in a million,' Elaine said. 'A Guy in a hundred million – a Guy in – ? How many hundreds or thousands of millions or billions of men are there in the world? But there's only one Lord Mayor of London!'

'And there's only one Guy married to you – ' He tried to capture her, but she eluded him, laughing.

'Not now,' she said. 'Today you belong to the City of London. But tonight – ' Her hand brushed his chin softly, a caress and a promise. 'Tonight, you'll belong to us – to me – again.'

'I wish you could come with me in the coach,' he said. 'All of you.'

'And flout five centuries of tradition?' She laughed. 'The City of London is a male chauvinist pig stronghold – we all know that. Perhaps you'll be able to make a dent in that tradition – but not this minute. Not before you're even sworn in. Don't worry, we'll be thinking of you all along the way. We'll be with you every moment, whether you see us or not.'

'I'll blow you a kiss,' he said. 'Especially for you and the children. You're going to be watching from the windows of – '

'No.' She shook her head. 'I know we have reserved seats, but we won't use them. I'm going to take Geraldine and Timothy out along the route and we'll mingle with the crowds. This is a once-in-a-lifetime thing, after all. I want them to remember it. Not just as another stuffy occasion amongst a lot of old fogies. I want them to be out in the middle of it all, watching the world cheer their father. How many children can ever have memories like that?'

'Elaine – ' This time she didn't escape him, but nestled softly in his arms for a moment.

'I'll go and bring in Geraldine and Timothy now.' Gently, she released herself. 'They'll want to see you – ' she handed him the plumed hat – 'in all your fine feathers before you get into the coach. After that, we'll slip out the back door and then we'll dodge in and out of the crowds all along the way. We ought to be able to see you at a dozen places if we walk fast enough. It will be a day none of us will ever forget.'

She smiled once, over her shoulder, and went to fetch the children.

Lucky Guy. The one without luck had been the poor Korean who had strayed farther afield just as they reached the other side of the minefield. Until then, Guy hadn't been aware of how closely and tightly the rest of them had been following in his footsteps.

The explosion had been a bolt out of hell. The blast had knocked most of them off their feet, torn some clothes off a few – but killed no one except the Korean. Expendable, in their viewpoint.

Guy had never let the others know how thoroughly it had shaken him. They drank with him that night and toasted him; later, they had volunteered for his patrols, fought to go on furlough with him. Perhaps they had been right – every one of them had survived while, all around them, others had died.

Fortunately, Guy had never talked or cried out in his sleep, so none of them could have guessed the recurring nightmare which woke him time and again in the blackest hour before dawn. Once again, the makeshift platoon had rallied around him; once again, he had begun leading them across the minefield; but this time he had known what lay ahead. Not for some hapless Korean this time. This time there was a special bomb lying in wait for him. He always awoke just as he put his foot on it, just as he experienced the terrible knowledge that there was a lump beneath his foot that should not have been there, that he had betrayed the men who had trusted him, leading them to death rather than safety –

Racked with shudders, drenched in sweat, he used to awake trying to call out vainly to his men to go back . . . to run . . . to duck . . . to save themselves. It was too late for him. Yet, knowing deep down that it was too late for them, as well.

Lucky Guy . . . lucky Guy . . . lucky Guy . . . It resounded over and over in his head like a litany during those first few moments of awakening when he fought back to the realization that it had only been a dream, a nightmare, that he was safe in a warm bed, his war long over, his battles won, his men safe.

All his battles were boardroom battles now and, even there, he won. Even there, they recognized and responded to the legend. It helped that he constantly made the right decisions – or was that just luck again? As it had been from the first.

'*People will always have to eat.*' He had quoted his

grandmother's favourite saying at the platoon's farewell party before they were all shipped back to their respective countries, when the talk had inevitably turned to what they were going to do back in Civvy Street. He had never thought about it especially before – it had been enough just to survive. But now it appeared that they all had a future to begin thinking about.

'*People will always have to eat,*' he had said impulsively, knowing that his decision had suddenly been made for him as he heard himself speak. He looked around at his men, his ex-men, and saw more than one of them nodding acknowledgement. It had been a heady – and faintly unnerving – experience to know that they were still going to follow his lead, even into civilian life.

He had started with a small speciality shop, importing the foreign foods that people grew accustomed to when fighting, or serving, in foreign territory. Filling, cheap viands in their own home grounds became exotic expensive delicacies when imported. The shop had done so well that he had opened another, and another, broadening his range until, finally, he had found himself with a chain of supermarkets on his hands. But the sense of borrowed time remained, the feeling that he owed something to someone, somewhere, for having been spared when so many were not. For being a Lucky Guy. With a sense almost of repaying a debt, he had always allotted a generous portion of his time to charity work. And that had been lucky for him, too. That was where he had found Elaine.

The years and honours had rolled along: member of the Worshipful Company of Grocers, Alderman of the City of London, Sheriff, a Knighthood, and now, the culmination, more than he would ever have dared dream of – lying muddy and wet in a Korean field – Lord Mayor of London.

And, over the years, the reports had come in from the others. Ernie had gone back to New York City and opened a delicatessen which had attracted growing popularity and eventually turned into one of the big showplace restaurants of the city, patronized by sports and theatrical celebrities – and the fans who wanted to glimpse them. Mack had opened a hamburger stand in Vancouver, used the extra land behind it to build a motel and wound up with a coast-to-coast chain of motel-and-hamburger stands almost before he could turn around. Peter had done something similar in Australia. In New Zealand, Geoff had opted for farming – and never looked back. The others had done well, all successful to a greater or lesser degree, and all occasionally mentioned that they felt they owed some of it to him; 'Guy's luck' was still holding good – and when was he going to come and visit and let them repay in hospitality at least something which could never really be repaid?

It might be fun, at that. Just to take Elaine and the children and do a round-the-world trip, stopping off to visit them all. Why not? When his year of office was over, he would have to remain out of the social swing for a year in order not to cramp the next Lord Mayor's style. It would be an ideal way of keeping out of sight and yet not losing any time. It would be the easiest way for him to keep out of City affairs, and yet he could renew old friendships, perhaps make new contacts, and generally widen his horizons. It was going to be a wonderful experience to be Lord Mayor of London but it wasn't the be-all and end-all of existence. There was a world and a future beyond it.

But that was in the future. He stretched luxuriously, then settled his chain of office again. There was this year in office to be enjoyed first. And right now, the parade. The Lord Mayor's Show to open his year in office.

He crossed to the window. Outside Guildhall, the crowds were thick and colourful everywhere you looked. From the other side of the street, where fascinated and awed spectators stared up at Guildhall or down at the ornate carriages waiting outside the door, to the rooftops all along the street, there was a solid mass of bustling joyous humanity – most of them children. It was a day for children; even the adults became children for the time it took the parade to pass. They might not be as vocal, nor wave tiny Union Jacks with wild enthusiasm, but they were there and they were prepared to have a good time.

And so was he! It was *his* day, after all. Guy glanced anxiously skyward, the occasional gleams of weak sunlight seemed to have disappeared with the advancing morning. The sky was now grey, but clear. Would the weather hold? Would 'Guy's luck' extend that far? Childish, perhaps, to cross one's fingers, but he did so. Everyone was a child today.

'*Don't rain on my parade* . . .' he hummed tunelessly, but fervently, then heard himself and laughed aloud. But he hummed the refrain again, as much of a prayer as he dared bother the Almighty with, after everything else that had been vouchsafed to him. '*Don't rain on my parade* . . .'

A hail from beneath the window brought his attention back to earth. He looked down and waved to Barney, in costume, capering below.

Barney – the only other Londoner in the platoon – who now owned six of the finest bakery shops in Greater London. Barney's Bakeries, beloved by every gourmet and widely patronized by the general public as well. Barney could easily have opened more shops – a baker's dozen of them, at least – but he preferred not to grow too large, to remain in a position to control the quality output of the shops he already ran. And it was not as though he needed the money, the existing shops brought him a generous profit.

Barney was combining a couple of nursery rhymes for his theme for the day. Dressed as a chef, with towering white hat, he carried an enormous papier mâché pie, divided into sections, the tops of which could be pulled back to release 'Four-and-twenty blackbirds'. Blackbirds which would flutter into the air by means of a rubber band and match-stick arrangement glued to the blackbird silhouette. Behind Barney would walk Young Guy, his son, dressed as Simple Simon and carrying more papier mâché pies, so that the children all along the route would have a chance of catching a blackbird – which would then be exchanged at one of Barney's Bakeries for a genuine pie.

Guy grinned. It was going to be handout day for the kiddies. Even Clover the TV clown had decided to get in on the act and was going to be throwing out tickets to his TV shows. Sure, those tickets were free anyway, but a lot of parents wouldn't take the time and trouble to write in for tickets, whereas, if they were delivered straight into childish hands, they would have no peace unless they actually took the kids to the TV programme.

They were all jumping on the bandwagon of his original idea of handing out black cat tokens to the children, but he didn't mind. By now, he was so accustomed to people clinging to his coat-tails for luck that he would have worried if they had not been there. Now, even the City of London was trying to cash in on Guy's luck.

Well, let them. His coat-tails were long, he had luck enough for everyone. Let them all cling on.

Guy grinned again and waved expansively to Barney.

Barney, in a burst of exuberance, tipped back the triangular top of one of the sections, catapulting a swarm of blackbirds upwards towards the window before they fell fluttering back to earth to be snatched up eagerly by the children nearby.

Across the room, a door opened. Guy heard and turned to face his family, to preen before them. This was *his* day. He was Lucky Guy.

It was years now since he had last had that nightmare about crossing the Korean minefield.

It was more than a decade since he had last been haunted by the feeling that some day his luck might run out, that somewhere a bomb was lying in wait for him.

CHAPTER IV

'Why don't you *do* something?' Maureen O'Fahey lifted a face bloated and ravaged by tears, her voice rising to a shriek. 'Why are you all standing around bedevilling me? Haven't I told you everything? Why do you have to keep asking questions over and over again? Why aren't you all out *doing* something?'

She couldn't be blamed for her attitude, Woman Police Constable Hilary Hendon thought, surveying the Irish girl dispassionately. It must appear to her that nothing whatever was being done. She could not know the forces she had already set in motion, nor the forces still being held in reserve. It must seem to her as though these dubious, constantly-questioning people had not moved since she had first told them her story.

'It's all right,' Hilary soothed. 'Believe me, we *are* doing something. Here, try to drink a little coffee – you'll feel better.' (Since they had poured a double measure of brandy into it, she ought to. If she drank all of it, it might calm her down enough to allow her to answer the still more delicate questions which remained to be asked.)

'Coffee!' Maureen O'Fahey struck out at the proffered drink, knocking the cup out of Hilary's hand and sending the liquid splashing across the desk to trickle uselessly on to the floor. (So much for that bright idea.) 'How can anyone think of coffee at a time like this? I'm asking you – why don't you *do* something? Why did I come here?' Her head drooped, only dry sobs came now, there were no more tears left. 'Why am I wasting my time here? We haven't *got* that much time!'

'We *are* doing something,' Hilary assured her again. It would be tactless to be more specific. A more sophisticated woman might suspect that they had to check out her story before they could do too much. Anyone could walk into a police station and make baseless accusations. Many people had. The police acted at their peril if they moved to arrest or impede citizens who must be assumed innocent until proved – or fairly certainly suspected of being – guilty.

'Then where's my Kitty? ! ! ?' Eyes blazing, Maureen O'Fahey challenged them. 'Why haven't you found her? Brought her back to me? *If* you're doing so much work! !'

It was unanswerable. Especially as complications added to the delicacy of the situation. *Miss* O'Fahey might not realize that it was not unknown for a woman to try to exact revenge upon a former lover by lying to the police about him. If the father of her child had innocently taken that child out for a treat, there was even a certain type of mentality which would report the incident to the police as a kidnapping. The ensuing chaos, humiliation and disruption could then be justified as no more than was due to the man to pay him back for what he had done to her.

Especially in this neighbourhood, where domestic disputes were endlessly complicated by the wild, unfettered excesses of the Irish temperament. People disciplined only by the black threat of an inexorable Hereafter, during the eternity of which they would relentlessly be forced to expiate sins which more balanced people were able to forgive themselves and understand as being part of nature rather than deliberate revolt against the laws of a vengeful God. Being convinced that she had committed the worst sin of all, Miss O'Fahey appeared to be particularly vulnerable to such inner pressures. Perhaps, if time allowed, it might be as wise to bring down her parish priest to take over his share of the situation.

Meanwhile, two policemen were at the O'Fahey lodgings, chatting up the landlady in an attempt to sweet-talk their way into certain rooms without an official search warrant. (Not the easiest thing to organize on a Saturday morning with no Court in session and no evidence on which to base an application.)

They would also talk to and sound out the opinions of as many of the other lodgers as they found available. Again, operating under the difficulties caused by its being Saturday, when most people were either out shopping, or away for the weekend.

Shopping. Hilary suppressed a sigh. That was what *she* had intended to be doing this afternoon. Technically, she was off duty. However, she had made the tactical error of stopping in to collect a sweater she had left in her locker before going on to the West End to look at a suit she had seen advertised at Selfridges. But she had found herself immediately swooped on and placed on duty. Because Saturday evening, especially after the pubs had closed, was the busy time around here, only a skeleton staff was on duty Saturday mornings. The rest of them reported on duty for the night shift.

Hilary hadn't even been given time to change into uniform. Her harassed male colleagues had tossed her sweater back in her locker and pushed her into the front office where she had been confronted with Maureen O'Fahey and asked to determine the truth or otherwise of the story O'Fahey was telling.

She still wasn't sure. Like the rest of them, she supposed, she didn't really *want* to believe it. The implications were too appalling. The whole idea was a nightmare – but so much of what people could do to each other was a nightmare. Man's inhumanity to man was an understatement of the facts that prevailed.

The police were more accustomed to it than most. But even they quailed at this one.

A standby alert had gone out, just in case it was true. Meanwhile, the checking-out process continued and the cross-questioning went on.

'Where is the child's father, Miss O'Fahey?'

'He emigrated. To Australia on an assisted passage. He said he'd send for us – after the baby was born – and send us money the while. But he was lying.' Her head lifted challengingly. 'I never heard from him again.'

'Why should this man, this Mike Carney, want to do such a thing?'

'How do I know? He must be mad. I never talked to him but to pass the time of day. I had no way of knowing how insane he was down deep inside. It didn't show all that much on the surface.'

'You say, "all that much". What do you mean by that?'

'Well, he was odd. But lots of people are odd without being downright crazy.'

'Odd in what way?'

An intercom buzzed on a desk in the corner. The questioner answered it, spoke briefly, and left the room. Another policeman took up the questioning.

'Odd in what way?'

'Oh, lots of ways,' she said vaguely. 'Like, you'd be talking to him of a morning and not ten minutes later he'd pass you by in the street as though he'd never seen you before. Looking inward, sort of.'

'Mmm.' The questioning officer evidently mirrored Hilary's private opinion that this was not terribly unusual. It hardly rated as circumstantial evidence. 'Anything else?'

'You're wasting time!' she stormed. 'Why aren't you out finding Kitty? What good do questions do?'

'Yes, yes,' he said. 'Believe me, we're doing everything we can. But we need your help, too. Now tell me, have you ever heard him mention the Sinn Fein – or the IRA?'

'No, not that I recall. I've been telling you. We didn't talk all that much, him and me. He hardly talked to anybody at all.'

'You mean he hadn't any friends?'

'That's what I'm saying. He wasn't the friendly sort.'

'What about his workmates? Other people in the house? Perhaps people he met at the pub? He must have known someone.'

'Oh, *known*. That's different. You didn't say *known* before, you said *friends*.'

Hilary stifled another sigh, the questioning officer looked as though he were stifling a great deal more

than that. It had been this way all through the
questioning. Miss O'Fahey seemed to be distress-
ingly literal. She answered strictly in accordance
with the exact question and admitted no interpreta-
tion of any wider aspects the question might have.
Before long, they might start wondering whether this
were deliberate on her part.

'Then – ' he continued with carefully controlled
impatience, 'can you tell me who *knew* him?'

'Well, I don't know about who might know him
at the pub, but where we live, there's Pat Donovan,
for a start. It was Pat as got him the room at the
house. They work together and, when he was new –
a year or so ago – Pat brought him back because
he didn't have anywhere to stay. Pat was – ' Her
voice broke suddenly. 'Pat was *sorry* for him.'

'Quite so.' The cool voice fought against en-
croaching emotionalism. 'That's a start. Where do
they work?'

'Didn't I tell you?' She looked up, startled. 'They
work for the demolition company.'

One wasn't aware of the amount of background
noise in the room until it all stopped abruptly.

'Demolition,' he echoed flatly.

The spell broke; the recording officer began noting
the words in his shorthand pad again, the faint hum
of conversation across the room took up once more,
even the telephone began to ring. But there was a
new urgency underlying it all. Suddenly the story
Maureen O'Fahey had been insisting on had
descended from the realms of fantasy into the region
of distinct possibility.

'That's what I've been saying.' Her face flushed
as she began turning belligerent. 'Can't you get it

through your heads? Won't you believe me and stop standing there and get out and *do* something?'

'We're doing all we can,' he said mechanically. Someone else had answered the telephone and was frowning. 'But we need your help. We *must* have your help.'

'There he is!' She raised her voice, pointing at the man who had just entered with the two worried-looking police constables. 'That's him!'

The man recoiled slightly, as though suspecting a paternity charge was being lodged against him, then pulled himself together and hurried forward.

'Maureen,' he said. 'What's going on here? What the devil is this all about?'

'That's Pat Donovan,' she affirmed, still pointing, although he had moved within touching distance of her finger. 'That's him, as ever was. You ask him why he brought that monster into our house!'

'Maureen – what's the matter?'

Another man entered the room, carrying a portfolio. He made his way unerringly towards the group.

'Now, Miss O'Fahey,' the questioner smiled. 'We'll need a description of this man – ' His cheerful tone refused to admit that they had already covered this territory to no avail. 'We realize that it's difficult to describe someone when you're not used to doing so. That's why we've evolved the Photofit. Now, if you'll just look at these pictures and tell us – '

'Pictures!' She exploded. 'Look at pictures? At a time like this! Are all the English mad? Don't you know what I've been saying – ?' She was on her feet, gripping her handbag as though to lash out with it. 'Are all of you insane?'

Involuntarily, they fell back slightly as she advanced. Hilary slipped to one side, but kept pace with her advance. There was no telling which way this cat would jump.

'Please, Miss O'Fahey.' Her questioner moved to block her, speaking gently, reasonably. 'We realize this must seem time-wasting, perhaps useless, to you but, believe me, it *is* essential.'

'I'm leaving,' she announced, having stopped listening to his protests. 'You're no good at all – the lot of you!'

'No, please – '

'Yes!' She cut him off. 'The only way you can keep me here any longer is to arrest me. Do you want to do that?'

'We're asking for your co-operation.' He tried a tone that was close to pleading. 'We need to build up a picture of the man we're looking for. So if you'll just look at these pictures – '

'You're just trying to humour me, that's what you're doing. Do you think I don't know?' Her eyes flashed fire and sparks seemed to shoot out from the dark red hair.

'No, I assure you – ' He kept out of range. He had seen Irish tempers and he had seen red-headed tempers – he had no wish to collide with a mixture of the two.

'Don't bother!' She swept past him, blazing with fury. 'I'll find Kitty myself!'

'Maureen – ' The man called Donovan tried to stop her, but she brushed him away, running now that she was breaking clear of them all.

Hilary caught up her shoulder bag and dashed after Maureen O'Fahey, vaguely aware that Donovan had said something to her colleagues which had stopped them in their tracks.

She caught up with Maureen O'Fahey just as the woman flagged down a taxi and stepped inside, giving her destination tersely.

Hilary wrenched open the door and flung herself inside, landing with a thump on the seat beside the O'Fahey woman as the taxi pulled away from the curb and hurtled in the direction of the City.

'It's all right,' Hilary said quickly, to forestall any protest. 'I'm here to help you. Really, I am.'

She need not have bothered. Having got thus far, Maureen O'Fahey had collapsed in a corner of the taxi, leaning back against the seat, her face drained of all emotion, all colour. All the fight had gone out of her.

'You can't help.' She opened a lacklustre eye, turning it towards Hilary unseeingly. 'No one can.' The dry retching sobs shook her body again. 'It's all over.'

CHAPTER V

'Look, Uncle Mike! Look, Da!' Kitty jerked at his hand, bouncing up and down with excitement, pointing wildly. 'Look! Donkeys! Are they going to give rides? Can I have a ride on them?'

'Take it easy!' He tried to hold her down. Did all kids jounce around like this? 'No, they're not giving rides – they're part of the parade. Don't jump! Don't point! Didn't anybody ever tell you you shouldn't behave like that? Where were you brought up – in a barn?'

'Noo-o-o.' She considered it momentarily. 'I'd *like* to live in a barn. Why can't we? Why can't people live in barns?'

'Because they can't, that's all!' He was aware of amused smiles all around them, of too much attention being concentrated on them. Why couldn't the brat shut up? Why couldn't she be still? What had gone wrong? He'd never envisioned the kid acting like this. Just a quiet little kid, doing what she was told, carrying the can – that was what he had planned.

Too late, he'd realized that nothing about her was quiet. There were even leather-saving metal tips on the toes and heels of her shoes which gave her a clicking clattering walk to call attention to her even when her high-pitched little voice was still.

'Let's go closer! I want to *see* them better!' She tugged imperatively at his hand and nearly slipped out of his grasp.

'Easy,' he said, trying for a jovial tone. 'Easy.'
There were too many watching eyes, listening ears.
He forced himself to smile down at her. Under his
breath, he cursed. His hands were slippery with
sweat and she had nearly twisted loose from him.
What would he do if she were to get away? That
was something he hadn't thought of before. If she
disappeared into the crowd, how would he ever find
her again? One kid amongst so many. Damn her!
Damn her! Why had he placed himself in a position
where he was so dependent on her?

Because she would never be suspected. That was
why. Because he could take her anywhere along the
route, push her to the front, and no one watching
would think twice about it. She was his safe-conduct
through any lines of suspicion and into the enemy
territory he hoped to decimate. He had to keep her
with him.

'*There*! Look *there*!' She twisted like an eel in his
grasp, carried away by the excitement of actually
witnessing the sort of scenes that heretofore she had
only seen on a television set – and black and white
at that. 'Oh, *look*!'

'Yes, yes. Wait a minute.' He grasped her round
the wrist with his other hand while he disengaged
the hand she had been holding and rubbed it up
and down on his jacket, trying to dry the perspiration. Then he took her hand again in a tight
renewed grasp. She must not slip away.

'Over there – ' She tugged, but he was able to
keep better hold of her now. 'There's a band!'

'There are lots of bands.' He looked around
sourly. They were up by London Wall and every

street turning held marchers, floats, bands, and assorted dignitaries, waiting for the signal to begin the parade. They would feed out of these turnings at the blast of a whistle, the wave of a baton, and fall into line behind each other until they merged going down Wood Street and were in formation as they passed Guildhall and picked up the final coaches full of dignitaries which would wind up the parade. Circuses, if not bread, for the masses.

The Lord Mayor's Show.

'Oooh, *look*!'

They had rounded one corner too many. The Army stood waiting. At ease, but ready to snap into action: carrying rifles; manning rocket launchers; on foot in marching order; sitting in camouflaged Land-Rovers with machine-guns mounted at the back; there was even a tank, monstrous and implacable, ready to roll and crush everything in its path.

For one constricted moment, he felt that they *knew*, that they were waiting here for him. That – at any instant – all eyes would turn towards him, identifying him, recognizing him, hating him as he hated them. Hatred a living palpable thing between them. That they would begin to march, to roll, to rumble forward, inexorably coming towards him and for him, to crush him, flatten him, grind him into the earth and so finish off another enemy – as they had finished off so many.

'Back – !' He yanked at her arm, nearly jerking her off her feet with the force expended. 'Get back!'

'You *hurt* me.' She looked up at him, eyes brimming with tears compounded equally of pain and angry recrimination. 'Don't *do* that! You *hurt* me.'

He'd like to kill her! The stupid little cow. Seduced, like all of them, by the smiling faces, the way the soldiers waved to the kids, swapped jokes with each other, lit their cigarettes and laughed – oh, all the stupid females fell for it.

Like Mary. He hadn't meant to think of her, not today, but now that he had, all the grievances came rushing back into his mind. And why shouldn't he think of her today? Wasn't she the inspiration for all this? Her with her soft lying lips and sparkling deceitful eyes, promising everything – giving nothing. At least, not to a man who'd worked to earn it.

His Mary. No, not his, in the end. Promised to him, planning a future with him, flat-hunting and saving money in a joint account. Well, perhaps she'd put more in than him, but that was only natural because he earned less, he'd been going to put a great big deposit into the account, when he'd had a win on the horses, or something, and see her eyes light up and hear her tell him he was wonderful.

Only then the Army unit from London came to town. Them with their talk about the Big City and their lah-di-dah accents and the girls falling all over themselves to chase after them. *But not his girl.* That was what he'd thought, fool that he'd been.

Until he'd had a letter in the post – she'd not had the guts to face him with it. And, when he went to the bank, he'd found out why. Cleaned out – account closed. *Women, they were all alike. They all deserved to die!*

'Da – ' The tug at his hand was uncertain. 'Da, are you all right? You look funny.'

Nothing funny about it. And nothing funny about all

these screaming brats and their stupid uniform-loving thick heads. *But this one was dead – or as good as.* He had almost forgotten that.

'Sorry. I was just being absent-minded, like, for a minute.' He smiled down at her, feeling kindly now. She was never going to grow up into an un-thinking little slut like the rest of them. *Not this one – she was finished.* 'But we're going the wrong way. We want to go over here – '

'But I want to see the soldiers – *oh!*'

It was still military, but it was a band around this corner. They were still in the hated uniform, but powerless. Nothing more dangerous than a slide trombone here; nothing more deadly than the weighted baton the leader swung. This was a lot more like it.

'See?' He swung her hand triumphantly. 'Isn't this better? Look at the trumpets and drums – they'll make a fine noise.' *But not as fine as the noise you'll make, little lady, before much more time has passed.*

'Ye-es . . .' She sent him a guarded, wary look, as though she had sensed the hostility behind his smiling mask. Her face was thoughtful as she turned it away from him to look at the colourful brass band.

'And will you just see who's coming along the street now – a flag seller. You said you wanted a flag, didn't you? And you shall have one.' He was openly wooing her now, fearful that someone might have observed the earlier slip into brutality, perhaps noted it mentally, to be remembered later – when the police began appealing for information. When they released their pictures and sketches labelled,

'Have you seen this child?' He beamed down at her anxiously. 'You *do* want a flag, don't you?'

'Ye-es . . .' It seemed to be against her better judgement, but the agreement came. Who would notice the hesitation – in a child?

Certainly not the flag seller, who beamed as he bestowed the Union Jack on Kitty, pushing it into her shyly outstretched hand.

'There you are,' Mike said. 'And look – here comes the programme seller, too. We want a programme, don't we?'

He didn't wait for her agreement as he beckoned the programme seller to them. The official programme was vital. It would give the order of the marchers, the route of the march and, more importantly, the time when the parade reached each major point on the route. Once he had that, he could then work out the final timings for himself – beginning the timing here at the start of the parade – and discover, within a minute or two, the exact moment when the Lord Mayor's coach would reach any given point along the route.

Kitty reached out for the programme as he paid the seller, and he repressed a curse as the seller delivered the programme into her hands. *Greedy little cow – did she have to grab everything?*

'Here – ' He fumbled the change the programme seller had given him back into his pocket and reached for the programme. 'Let me see that.'

'I'm *reading* it,' she said haughtily, keeping it just beyond his grasp.

'You can't read.' About to snatch it from her, he was aware of an amused bystander watching them. He ground his teeth and forced a smile.

'You're too little to read. Now, give it to Da,
there's a good girl. You can have it back again
as soon as I see what I want in it.'

'You promise?' She slanted an upward glance at
him, still half-mistrusting his sudden wooing. Then
her eyes moved beyond him, catching the amusement on the onlooker's face and her own face
shuttered – children hate being laughed at. 'Take
it then.' She thrust it at him and ducked her head
down, either shy or sulking.

'That's fine.' One-handed, he slipped it open,
silently cursing the awkwardness of it, but not
daring to let go of her hand. If she should take it
into her head to dash off into the crowd, they were
both lost.

There it was, the Order of Procession – that was
what he wanted. Frowning, he scanned the pages.
Three pages before the Lord Mayor's coach was
listed, three pages encompassing bands, floats,
military units, more bands, more floats, the officers
of the Worshipful Companies of the City, carriages
of City dignitaries, separated by yet more bands and
military units – the list seemed to go on endlessly.
How long would it take them all to pass by?

And which was the Army unit they had just
backed away from? He hadn't stayed long enough
to get a clear view of the uniform markings or regimental insignia – not that he'd especially be able
to interpret them if he had seen them. They were
all soldiers – that was the only important point. It
was too bad he couldn't blow them all to hell, but
he hadn't enough explosive – not here, not now.
He had to concentrate on the most important
target – the big-wig who'd make the loudest bang.

What time did the Lord Mayor's coach pass?

Ah, there it was. Over on the other page, beside the 'Route of Procession'. Down at the bottom. *'Thereafter the times for the passing of the Lord Mayor's coach are approximately 30–35 minutes after the head of the procession.'*

The procession was headed – and ended – he noted, by the City of London Police. Much good it would do them.

From somewhere down the line, a whistle sounded. And then another. The short, warning blasts resounded from street to street like endless echoes, signalling. And the marchers raised their heads, suddenly alert.

Last drags were taken on cigarettes and then cigarettes were ground out underfoot. People waved to each other and began to move swiftly and purposefully, climbing up on to floats. Others jumped alert, shifting into military formation in the centre of the street, suddenly becoming formidable mobile units rather than faintly sloppy individuals out for a day's amusement.

Even the animals seemed to snap into alertness, catching the atmosphere roiling around them. Heads lifted, ears flicked, feet stamped restlessly, ready to move forward.

'Da – Uncle Mike – Da – ' Kitty tugged urgently at his hand. 'They're *starting*!'

'Da!' He snapped the correction automatically, still half occupied with working out the timing.

'Da – ' Tears quivering in her eyes, she attempted to placate him. 'Da, we'll *miss* it if we don't – '

'Stop fussing! We won't miss a thing. It goes on for hours.'

'But I want to see it *all*!' Her head turned anxiously as she tried to monitor the activity on all sides, the scenes of imminent departure fuelling her restiveness.

'You will,' he promised. *Oh, how you will!* 'Just be quiet another little minute and let me work out the best way for us to go.'

He turned back to the programme, searching urgently for the information he needed. *There!* The Lord Mayor boarded his coach in Gresham Street and proceeded to Mansion House where he took the salute. *Salute and be damned to the English bastard!*

After that, the procession would continue along the route as scheduled. Until he met the unscheduled event. *Until he took an Irish salute.*

'Come on.' He rolled the programme into a cylinder, clutching it tightly. 'This way.'

'But everybody else is going *that* way.' She seemed determined to give him an argument at every turn. But there were still too many people around to clout her.

'That's why we want to go *this* way. It will get us out of the crowd and we'll be able to move faster. You want to get to the best place to watch the parade, don't you?' *The place where an explosion could be counted on to have the most devastating effect.*

'Oh, yes,' she agreed happily.

'Come on, then.' He smiled down at her, equally happy.

United in sudden enthusiasm, they moved off into the crowd, beaming at each other.

CHAPTER VI

'Let her go,' Donovan said. 'I can describe him as well as she can. Perhaps better.'

At a nod from the commanding officer, the other policemen relaxed and fell back.

'Hilary's still with her – ' From the window, one of them reported. 'Got into the taxi as it drove off. She can cover that end.'

'Look – ' Donovan said. 'Answer me just one question, will you? You're after Mike, all right? But what the devil has he done?'

'Nothing – yet.' At a nod from their superior, the two policemen who had escorted Pat Donovan to the police station moved forward.

'Look – ' Donovan glared at them. 'There's all of you swooping down like a wolf on the fold. There's Maureen half out of her mind. There's a Photofit man standing here champing at the bit. Stop taking me for a fool, man! I'm asking you and I want an answer – what the bloody hell is going on?'

'Mr Donovan – ' The commanding officer sighed deeply and seemed to fight for the energy to continue. 'Mr Donovan, do you know what day this is?'

'Saturday – ' Donovan looked at them blankly, sensing the incompleteness of this answer. 'It's Saturday. What's that got to do with it?'

'Correct, Mr Donovan. And what *other* day is it?'

Donovan frowned, visibly perplexed. What more of an answer was required from him? His face brightened. 'It's November – ' he said. 'November tenth – the day before Remembrance Sunday. Is that what you mean?'

'No.' The officer frowned, in his turn. 'Saturday, the tenth of November,' he intoned portentously. 'Doesn't that convey anything else to you?'

'Should it?' Donovan was nonplussed. A guilty man could not have dissembled so expertly.

'The tenth of November,' the officer prompted. 'How long have you lived in London?'

'Nearly ten years – ' Donovan looked at him suspiciously. 'What *is* all this?'

'And you still don't know what happens in November?'

'Well . . . usually . . .' Donovan groped visibly for it. 'The Queen opens Parliament – but not on a Saturday, surely?'

'No, not on a Saturday,' the other man confirmed. 'But what *else* happens in November?'

'There's Guy Fawkes' Day.' Donovan grappled with bewilderment. 'But that's on the fifth – that's past. What are you driving at?'

'It's also the time when we have the Lord Mayor's Show – a Saturday in November. Does *that* convey anything to you?'

'Oh, that. Why should it? It's mainly for kids, isn't it? They come from all over for it. It's a treat for the kiddies.'

'Precisely, Mr Donovan.'

Pat Donovan stared at him, trying to wrest sense from the words. There was a message in there somewhere – a grim message. Or was he imagining it?

'Look – ' he said. 'I'm a simple man. You'd better

spell it out in words of one syllable.'

'Miss O'Fahey has a five-year-old child, we understand. A little girl called Kitty.'

'That's right.' But Donovan was shaking his head sideways, like a punch-drunk prizefighter who'd been dealt a devastating blow. 'What of it?'

'Your friend, Mike – '

'Not a friend, no.' The protest was automatic. 'More of an acquaintance, like. He's not my friend – I don't think he's anybody's friend. That's not to say anything against him – ' Donovan was quickly on the defensive. 'He's a loner, that's all. Some people are.'

'Quite so.' The cold eyes sent an uneasy chill through him. 'Then you wouldn't say that the man was a joiner? That he might, perhaps, belong to some illegal organization?' But the suggestion was half-hearted. If there were anything like that, the computer would have turned it up by now. A wonderful thing the computer, but it wasn't infallible. It only gave out what had been put into it. It could deal with known offenders – but it couldn't identify the unknown: the sleepers, the grudge-bearers, the nutters.

'I . . . wouldn't say so.' The reply was slow in coming, perhaps more considered than his previous reactions had been. 'Of course, I couldn't swear to anything. I didn't know him all that well.'

'It appears that no one did. At least, no one is willing to admit it now. And you – ' the tone whip-lashed suddenly. 'Do *you* belong to any organization? The IRA? The Red Flag? The Angry Brigade? The – '

'Hell, no!' Donovan was abruptly furious. 'I'm a plain honest citizen – believe it or not. I even pay my taxes – which pay *your* salary, I might remind you. And I want to know why you've dragged me down here. It's Saturday, as you keep on reminding me. I'm on my own time, and I'm giving it up voluntarily and of my own free will because your men asked me nicely. But if you're going to start – '

'Quite, Mr Donovan, quite so.' The officer placated hastily. This was no time for the tax-paying worm to turn. He had to be treated as an honest citizen until proved otherwise. He had to be handled with respect, with kid gloves. 'Just keep calm – '

'I am,' Donovan said and, curiously, he was. The idea was getting through to him slowly but with an overpowering persuasiveness. '*I've* never belonged to any of those kind of organizations, but you think, maybe, Mike – '

'We can't be sure.' Again, the words were too quick, too glib. 'But the possibility can't be ignored. Especially in view of – '

'Of what?'

'You're in the demolition business, too?' The man changed track again.

'I work for the same demolition company.' Donovan was wary. 'But what – '

'You have access to demolition equipment? Gelignite? Nitroglycerine? Other explosives, perhaps?' *He* was asking the questions.

'You could say that. But there isn't much of it around where I work. They keep that sort of stuff mostly for work in the country – blasting out old tree stumps, getting rid of boulders. You can't use it in the city much. We work mostly with the old iron ball, and picks and sledge-hammers.'

'But explosives *are* available?'

'If you know where to look for them, yes, I suppose so.' Donovan felt increasingly uneasy. The cold chill that was settling over him told him he really didn't want to know where all this was leading, but knowledge was being forced upon him. 'Do you mean you think – ?' He broke off, unwilling to put it into words.

'"If you know where to look",' the man echoed him. 'Would it be very difficult to find out where?'

'No, it couldn't be – ' He fought against belief, against the hints which, added together, were beginning to make their own grim sense. 'And Kitty, little Kitty – no wonder poor Maureen was distracted out of her mind. You mean that devil is holding Kitty as some kind of hostage?'

'We wouldn't say "hostage", Mr Donovan.' The man shook his head slowly. 'Hostages have a chance.'

'But then, what's he doing with her? Not – ?'

'Have you ever gone to the Lord Mayor's Show, Mr Donovan?' He barely paused for the denial. 'Most of us have been on duty for it at some time in our professional lives. We have a rota for public events and we take our turns. The Lord Mayor's Show is one of the year's big treats for the kiddies. That means a well-ordered crowd, good-natured, putting the kiddies first. They're mostly mums and dads, you see, or some close relatives and they've all got kids along. That means they pass the tiny ones along to the front so that they can see everything. I've seen strangers helping out when there's a woman alone with her kids and putting the kids on their own shoulders to watch the parade go by. It's one of the best-natured crowds we have in London all year. And God knows, they've been getting fewer every year – the people who are out for fun and not for some kind of demo.'

'And he's taken Kitty to that? And you think – ?' Donovan broke off.

'Whatever cause he thinks he's working for, he won't be doing it any good. Unfortunately, none of these fanatics seem to realize that until it's too late. And, by that time, it's too late for a lot of innocent bystanders, as well. Nice, decent people, who just came in to Town on a Saturday morning to give the kiddies a good time.'

'Jesus God!' Donovan burst out. 'Why doesn't the bugger just set fire to an orphanage?'

'He may do that, too – if we don't catch him in time.'

'Look – ' Donovan said. 'I knew he was odd – I didn't know he was raving mad! But – for anybody to try to do a thing like that – are you sure?'

One of the constables who had escorted him to the police station moved aside and Donovan was able to see what he had placed on the desk: a Thermos flask from a child's lunch box and the empty casing of an alarm clock.

'Jesus!' Donovan said again. This time it was a prayer. He was on his feet and moving towards the door, but the constables blocked him.

'The identification – ' one of them reminded.

'But, look – we can't waste time!' He now knew the desperation Maureen had felt. Like her, he wanted to dash out, get to the parade, and start looking for that bastard, Mike.

'We're doing everything we can,' he was assured. 'But we need a picture of the suspect. That's where it's up to you. Once we build up some sort of picture, we can circulate it and our men will have an idea of what to look for.'

'I know. I know.' Donovan allowed himself to be led back to his chair. The Photofit man spread a variety of disembodied features on small cards in front of him. He tried to force himself to concentrate. So much depended on him now.

And he was faintly suspect himself, he knew. He had heard the off-note in their voices, watched the signals their eyes had sent. They were not sure that they could trust him. Not just because he had been identified as an associate of Mike's, but because he was Irish. Because his accent was the accent of terrorists. No matter that it was also the accent of millions of honest, hard-working people who wouldn't dream of violence, no matter that it was likely to be the accent you heard murmuring comfort in the long dark watches of a hospital night. They were all suspect because of the guilty few.

'That's it!' Donovan indicated the heavy eyebrows that were closest to Mike's and watched the policeman place the card on a blank pad, the beginning of the build-up to an entire face.

'There ought to be more – ' Donovan said restlessly – 'more that I can do. As soon as this is finished, I want to get out there, to look for him myself – '

'Yes, of course,' the officer in charge murmured soothingly. 'But you *do* realize that the route of the procession covers about two miles and that there can be as many as half a million spectators? None of us can be much use alone. You're far more valuable here, helping us right now.'

It came to Donovan with a shock that *he* was the man he'd heard about so often in police reports. The man *'now helping the police with their enquiries'*. The enormity of the task they faced nearly overcame him.

'Why don't you call it off?' he shouted. 'Why let it go on? Disband the procession, send everybody home. Clear the whole area – you're quick enough to do that, other times.'

'Quite so, Mr Donovan.' The dry tone pointed up the fact that his latent hostility had been noted, that there was always the possibility that the Irishmen were sticking together in some sort of double-bluff. To cancel one of the biggest spectacles of the year on the mere threat of a bomb attack might be to leave themselves open to international derision, not to mention leaving the way open for any crackpot with a grudge to make a telephone call and cancel any event he had happened to take a dislike to.

'You're not going to do it, though, are you?' Donovan sank back in his seat and dejectedly contemplated an assortment of mouths.

'It isn't up to us alone.' A walkie-talkie crackled in a corner as though endorsing his remark. 'We've notified the City of London Police – the Show is in their bailiwick for most of the time. But the Lord Mayor's Show has been running for five centuries – and this won't be the first time it's gone on against a bomb threat.'

'But this is more than a threat,' Donovan protested. 'It's a reality! There's a madman out there with a bomb – '

The walkie-talkie crackled again and the officer looked across the room to receive a nod from its operator. He sighed heavily.

'In any case, Mr Donovan,' he said, 'it's too late. They're rolling.'

CHAPTER VII

Hilary slid her walkie-talkie surreptitiously out of her shoulder bag and murmured into it softly, checking back with headquarters. Her instructions, as she had assumed, were to stay with Maureen O'Fahey and report immediately if, by any chance, they spotted the suspect.

Probably there had been no need to worry about keeping the operation inconspicuous. Maureen O'Fahey was leaning back against the corner seat, eyes closed, lips moving silently. She seemed unaware that she was not alone.

'Where *exactly* do you want to go?' The driver pushed aside his glass partition. 'The Lord Mayor's Show covers a lot of ground.'

It did indeed. Hilary glanced at Maureen O'Fahey, who gave no sign of having heard. She was lost in some terrifying world of her own.

'Do you know where you want to go?' Hilary reached over and shook her gently. Had the woman any clue? Perhaps something once heard that might have lodged in her mind to come back to her now when she needed it? Or perhaps she might just blurt out the first thing that came into her head, something bearing no relevance to the missing child.

'Do you know where you want to go?' Hilary repeated urgently.

'The Show – ' Maureen O'Fahey opened her eyes and looked around the taxi wildly. 'The Lord

Mayor's Show.' She fell back against the seat and her eyes closed again, as though the strain of holding them open were too great.

Hilary sighed. It was up to her. Could she put herself into the mind of a mad bomber? Not really – not even headquarters could expect it of her. She sighed again.

'It starts up in the City – ' the taxi driver offered helpfully. He met her gaze with faintly puzzled sympathy.

The City . . . the Lord Mayor's Show . . . the Lord Mayor . . . Why not? It was as likely as anything else.

'Mansion House,' Hilary said firmly.

'Well . . .' the driver shrugged. 'We can try.'

Hilary settled back, watching the familiar landmarks move past until they became less familiar and then completely unidentifiable as the taxi began to wind through narrow City streets, taking short cuts to get them to their destination.

She was glad now that she hadn't had time to change into uniform. She could walk through the crowds at Maureen O'Fahey's side now and not be conspicuous. She realized, with a cold chill, that this might mean the difference between life and death for her if they should happen to confront their quarry unexpectedly.

'. . . shouldn't have done . . . sin . . . judgement on me . . . never should have . . . knew it . . .' Maureen O'Fahey's inner turmoil abruptly became audible, although she had neither moved nor opened her eyes again. 'Mortal sin . . . but Kitty . . . not *her* fault . . . judgement on *me* . . . oh, God . . . oh, God . . . oh, God . . .'

Hilary leaned forward and slammed shut the glass partition between them and the driver. It was impossible to tell from the neutral set of his shoulders whether he had heard the words. Certainly, he was in no position to make anything of the random phrases.

'It's all right,' Hilary soothed falsely. 'It's all right.' Nothing might ever be right for Maureen O'Fahey again. They both knew that.

'No-o-o,' Maureen moaned. 'Oh, God, no-o-o...'

It was a state of shock, Hilary realized. Maureen should be made to lie down, kept warm, given cups of hot sweet tea – and all sorts of impracticable things like that. There was not one single concrete, useful thing that could be done in the present circumstances.

'It's all right,' Hilary repeated helplessly. 'It will be all right.'

'It won't, you know.' Maureen O'Fahey's eyes opened, suddenly sharp and focusing, alert to an intolerable position. 'It won't. It's been wrong from the beginning. I know it. I've always known it. But I didn't think she'd be taken away from me in punishment. *That's* wrong – it wasn't *her* fault. She was the only innocent one. But they always told me, "The sins of the fathers –".'

'Stop it!' Hilary said sharply. 'Pull yourself together! This isn't any kind of punishment – '

'Then what is it?'

'These things happen. Not just to you, but to other people, too. People who – '

'People who *don't* deserve them!' Maureen O'Fahey's eyes met hers, snapping in anger, challenging her to a fight, as though she might find some release in battle.

'Talking like this isn't going to do any good.' Hilary was not prepared to debate Celtic metaphysics with her. 'It won't help Kitty any.'

'Oh, no, you're right. You're right. But what *can* help her now?' Maureen O'Fahey turned wildly, pressing herself against the window glass, staring out into the street as though she could find the child by the sheer force of her desire to.

At least it was better than having her lashing herself into hysterics within the close confines of the taxicab. Hilary drew a deep breath and leaned back in her own corner, keeping watch out of her own window, trying not to feel that the assignment was hopeless.

The crowds were thicker now, as they crept closer to the heart of the City. The density of traffic had also increased and the driving was trickier as cars jockeyed for every advantage, obviously trying to get through the bottlenecks before the streets were closed to traffic until the parade went past.

Once the main thoroughfares were closed, their chances of finding the child diminished. Instinctively, Hilary felt that while the crowds were mobile there was a better chance. Once they had frozen into clusters, folding in on each other, pushing together, one small child could be hidden and lost from sight entirely.

Until, of course, her presence became known suddenly – and violently. Her *late* presence.

Hilary turned towards Maureen. 'Have you – ?'

She had been going to ask if the girl had had anything to eat that morning. Something about the pale wan appearance made her suspect that Maureen was not unduly concerned about food at the best of times.

'Look!' Maureen O'Fahey stiffened, pointing out the window into the crowd. 'There she is! That's Kitty! My Kitty!' She began clawing at the door handle, oblivious to the fact that the taxi was still moving.

'Where?' Hilary tried to follow the direction of the pointing finger, restrain Maureen from leaping out of the taxi instantly, and rap on the glass partition to signal the driver to stop, all in the same moment.

'There! Plain as ever!' Maureen twisted away from the restraining hand. 'Can't you see her? There!'

On the pavement, a child with red hair skipped between her parents, swinging a little red lunch box. At least, a small girl skipped between a man and a woman. She wore a navy blue raincoat and white knee socks. The red hair – a cross between carrot and copper – curled almost shoulder length. All they could see of her from the taxi was the back view. Unless the child turned, they would not see her face. There were literally thousands of children from all over London and the Home Counties in the City today for the Lord Mayor's Show; it was inevitable that more than one of them would have red hair.

'Are you sure?' Hilary asked. There had been no mention of a woman in the case before.

'Do you think I don't know my own child?' Maureen O'Fahey whirled on her. 'Do you think I don't know every bone in her body? Every hair on her head?'

She sounded so positive that Hilary's doubt diminished. Surely a mother knew her own child. Just because preliminary information hadn't indicated that there was a woman working with the man, it didn't mean that there might not be one in the background – or that he couldn't have picked one up somewhere along the way. A child with a man and a woman would be less noticeable than a child with a man alone.

The taxi had slowed, more in deference to the traffic than because of Hilary's signal. She was just about to pull back the glass and order him to stop when she became aware that Maureen O'Fahey had slumped back in the seat beside her.

'Oh, God!' she sobbed. 'Oh, God, where's Kitty?'

The child outside had turned around to watch the progress of a flag seller who was plodding along in the gutter crying his wares. The child had a round pleasant face liberally sprinkled with freckles. Above her, her mother's face was a freckled replica of her own, with the same carrot-copper hair peeping in a fringe beneath her headscarf. Mother and daughter, there could be no mistaking them.

'Oh, God! Oh, God!' It seemed impossible, but Maureen O'Fahey had found still more tears to shed. 'It's all my fault! It's a judgement – '

'Stop that!' Hilary snapped. For a fleeting moment, she considered the classic treatment for hysteria, but that presupposed a certain amount of privacy. There was too much of a crowd outside; someone's attention was sure to be caught and held by what would look like two women brawling in a taxi. Nor was the driver likely to be unconcerned.

Even now, he was glancing back at them uneasily.

'Pull yourself together!' Below the level of the driver's vision, Hilary grasped Maureen's arm and shook her. 'We need all our wits about us. You can't help your child by having hysterics!'

'Oh, that's true. It's true. There's nothing and no one can help her now.' Maureen slid into a high-pitched keening. 'She's lost and gone to us all. Gone . . . gone . . . gone . . .'

Hilary tightened her lips against exasperation. She would only alienate the girl by being too brisk or too brusque with her. Suppose it were *her* child, innocent and trusting, walking with death by her side in a little red lunch box – would *she* be half so controlled as Maureen O'Fahey? She took a deep breath against the rush of blood to her head, the pounding of pulses which answered her hypothetical question.

The driver looked back over his shoulder again and shrugged as she met his eyes. 'Afraid this is as far as we go.' He nodded to the scene ahead where police were swinging barricades across the street. A huge crowd of people swarmed out from the pavement in the wake of the crossbars to range themselves as a second – human – barrier across the street.

'Nothing's going to move for at least an hour,' he said. 'You might as well get out and walk the rest of the way.'

'We'll do that, thanks,' Hilary said.

Maureen was already fumbling for the door release, her eyes searching the crowd despairingly. At least she appeared to have stopped crying, probably realizing that tears would only blur her vision and she needed every speck of clarity she could muster.

And luck. Lots of luck.

Hilary paid the driver and stepped out of the taxi just behind Maureen who, she was relieved to note, had paused to wait for her. It seemed to presage a burgeoning partnership feeling. Or possibly Maureen O'Fahey simply shrank from being entirely alone in this milling crowd of strangers.

'We'll never find her,' Maureen moaned. 'Never in all this world.'

'We must.' But Hilary looked around and found herself infected by Maureen's despair. There were children everywhere, as far as the eye could see.

Even worse, they all looked alike. Oh, they came in different shapes and sizes; some faces were freckled, some sallow and some red-cheeked; but there was a basic similarity to them all. Perhaps it was the innocence, the youth, the exuberance; or perhaps it was the intense air of expectancy that seemed to radiate from them.

Worse, far worse, they were nearly all dressed in navy blue school macs – a sensible precaution against the threatening rain, but one which was not going to make the task of identification any easier.

It was like looking across a meadow of daisies and being expected to pick out one particular daisy.

'She isn't here.' Maureen O'Fahey seemed to have regained some of her spirit, possibly revived by the fresh air. 'Not on this street. Hurry, let's try another. If we can get to the corner, we can look more ways at once.'

'All right.' Hilary hurried to keep up with her.

If they got separated in this mob, they might never find each other again. And Maureen O'Fahey was her only hope of finding the child.

At the corner, Maureen halted, turning slowly to quarter the view. Everywhere, there were children. The sight seemed to daze her. She turned to Hilary with a sound that was half-way between a sigh and a moan.

'So many,' she said. 'I never realized there'd be so many.' She looked about again and gave a despairing shrug. 'I thought it wouldn't be so hard.' Her lips stretched in a grimace that did not result in the smile intended. 'I thought knowing about the red lunch box would help.'

Hilary nodded, her own mouth quirking in rueful acknowledgement. Like the navy blue macs, the little red lunch boxes were ubiquitous. How could she have escaped noticing them before? But then, she had never been looking for them before. Although, in a vague way, she had been aware of references to them in shopping columns and advertising, she had never realized the way in which they had captured the imagination of the young, becoming both a symbol to them and a badge of belonging.

All the children were carrying little red lunch boxes this year. They had become one of the mysterious all-encompassing fads that periodically sweep across the kingdom of childhood, a passport without which they were not duly accredited members of the promised land. Like the children, the lunch boxes came in various shapes and sizes; like the children, they were omnipresent.

'Never mind.' Hilary tried to mask her sinking

heart. 'We'll find her. It's early days yet – ' She caught the words too late. They didn't have days in which to search. 'It's early yet,' she amended.

'And, sure, who's looking at old lunch boxes anyway?' Maureen's spirits rose again, they were buoying each other up. 'It's the head we'll see first. Her face and her hair. They can't change that.'

'That's right, her hair.' Hilary acknowledged the reminder gratefully. There wouldn't be all that many little girls with red hair.

CHAPTER VIII

'Put this on,' Da said. 'It looks like it might be going to rain.'

Kitty took the little yellow sou'wester and looked at it dubiously, pulling her other hand free, the better to examine it.

'Go ahead – ' He bit down on impatience. Were kids always so slow? He wanted to snatch it from her hands and ram it down over that flaming tell-tale hair, but was afraid such a move would evoke a howl of protest that would attract the attention of everyone within earshot.

'Hurry up,' he said. 'You don't want to miss the parade, do you?'

'No-o-o.' She finished inspecting the sou'wester and slowly settled it on her head. 'How does it look?'

'Fine. Beautiful.' God! – even at that age they wanted the mirrors, the admiration, the homage. What chance did a man have? 'You look terrific. It suits you. Now come on – ' He reclaimed her hand. 'Hurry up.'

'Can we see Clover?' The sou'wester was on and forgotten, she was now as impatient as he. 'Can we see Clover the Clown?'

'That's right,' he urged her on. 'If you're good, we can see Clover twice. If we hurry, we can see him up here as he's getting into the parade – and then we can nip round somewhere else and find ourselves the best spot to watch the whole procession. Clover

will be close to the end – just before the Lord
Mayor's coach.'

'Ohhhh!' She danced along beside him, tugging
at his hand. 'Hurry, Da, hurry. Let's see Clover
twice!'

'Good girl!' He quickened his pace. He wanted a
last check on as many of the floats and marchers as
he could see. He knew from the programme just
what their various positions were supposed to be,
but that wasn't the same as actually seeing them.

When you could see them, you really knew the
score. The programme didn't tell you how many
men were marching in each section of the parade
– and whether or not they carried arms. As for the
armoured transport, it was pretty certain that – for
safety's sake, in case of accident – the mortars
would not be loaded. A quick look as he had
hurried Kitty past some of them had revealed that
they were not even carrying shells. There was
nothing to worry about from that quarter.

In any case, they would all be helpless once the
bomb had gone off. The initial shock and confusion
would be so great that a man could easily slip
away unnoticed in the tumult.

The only ones who might have a chance of
catching him were the marchers – the foot soldiers.
But most of them were bandsmen. Lumbered down
with heavy or bulky instruments, they would have
little chance of pushing their way through a crowd
panicked not for itself but for its children. Pursuit
would be impossible, the attempt useless.

Apart from which, most of the marchers were in
the early part of the procession, spaced out between
the floats. They would be too far ahead to be able to

turn back in time to be of help when trouble erupted.

No, it was only the last part of the procession that need concern him. He had it memorized: a regimental band; Clover the Clown on his famous ancient pennyfarthing – no chance of pursuit through the milling crowds on that, even if the clown had enough guts; a few carriages with Aldermen and City dignitaries; another regimental band –

And then, the Lord Mayor of London. Lucky Guy himself.

And this was where his luck ran out.

CHAPTER IX

Standby.
   Red Alert.
   The warning went out. Swiftly the emergency services of a great city moved into *Standby* position.

Designated hospitals nearest the route – Guy's and Bart's – began recalling as many of their off-duty staff as could be reached. Contingency arrangements were put in hand for additional supplies of blood plasma to be rushed where necessary from other hospitals outside the emergency area.

The St John Ambulance Brigade mobilized more vehicles and additional ambulances pulled up behind the ones already on duty along the parade route. Attendants got out and carried the standby warning to surprised colleagues who were normally prepared to deal only with the usual fainting spectators, lost tearful children, and the occasional genuine emergency such as a heart attack or an epileptic fit.

A covey of helicopters took to the air with a brisk whirring, like a flock of pheasant suddenly flushed from cover. Two would hover along the route. Two more would make wide sweeps over the spider-web of streets comprising the Square Mile and adjoining territory, observers on the lookout for anything remotely suspicious.

From the Metropolitan Division, to Scotland

Yard, to the City of London Police, calling upon the extra floating resources of the Special Patrol Group, the police forces had moved into action.

Red Alert.

CHAPTER X

'You look lovely, darling!' Another dab of red on the nose, a streaking of blue along the corners of the mouth, and the amateur make-up artist stepped back to admire his own work.

'Less of that, Slade, or I'll have you on a charge of insubordination,' the new clown growled.

'Well, at least you can't accuse me of dumb insolence!' The make-up man darted in again, adding red triangles at the corners of the steely grey eyes and stepped back for the final time, abruptly serious.

'You're as ready as you'll ever be,' he said. 'Good luck, Peter.'

'Thanks, mate.' The mouth was taut beneath the painted smile. 'I only hope this is going to do some good. It's a right needle in a haystack we're looking for.'

Three constables, also dressed in the ill-fitting clown outfits hastily commandeered from a theatrical costumiers, nodded agreement. Pasted to the palms of the oversized white gloves they were wearing, they had passport-sized reproductions of the Photofit pictures built up from the information supplied by Pat Donovan. In the left palm, the child; in the right palm, the suspect. As usual, the pictures, so hastily duplicated and distributed, could fit hundreds along the parade route – and probably would. It was up to them to try to make a correct identification.

'Right – ' Detective-Sergeant Peter Lutterworth swung round to inspect his colleagues, wincing only slightly. He looked no better himself, he knew. But they weren't entering a beauty contest.

They were infiltrating the procession – 'inconspicuously', he thought wryly – as part of a quasi guard of honour for Clover the Clown. With a little last-minute reshuffling of the Order of Procession, they would be positioned just in advance of the Lord Mayor's coach. They were to keep their eyes open, act as much like genuine clowns as possible – and hope to God some of Lucky Guy's luck extended to them.

'Right – ' he said again and nodded. They would pass muster. All except for their feet. The floppy plastic clown shoes which had been part of the costumes were piled in the corner – unwanted. If they did spot anything suspicious, they were going to have to move, and move fast, unimpeded by fancy footwear. Their regular shoes peeped neatly and incongruously from beneath the ruffles at the end of baggy polka-dotted satin trousers. It was a small point and highly unlikely to be noticed. The children would be too excited, and all their attention would be centred on Clover and his pennyfarthing, anyway.

The quarry would have too much on his mind to worry about minor costume deficiencies. Probably he'd be in such a keyed-up state that any discrepancy he noticed, or imagined he noticed, might set him off. They were, in more senses than one, dealing with an unexploded bomb.

'You know what we have to do.' Lutterworth addressed the others. 'Any questions?'

'Who knows what's going on?' Constable Johnson, recognizable only to those who had seen the red fright wig being fitted, spoke. 'In the procession itself, I mean. Apart from Clover the Clown, that is?'

'*We* know.' Lutterworth's face was grim beneath the painted mask. 'And the military units have been alerted – they'll be keeping an eye out for anything that doesn't look right. Some of them have been marching in this Show for years, they might have a better chance than us of spotting it. If they do, they'll pass the word to the nearest policeman.'

'Not everybody in the Show knows, then?'

'Not the civilians. No need to worry them about something that may never happen.'

'And if it does – ?' One of the other men spoke.

'If it does, the chances are they'll be in the clear. Most of them are on the floats – professional models who've been hired for the day on PR budgets, or else amateur volunteers. They'll all be in the first three-quarters of the Show. Our chum is going to be concentrating on our bit of the programme.'

'Does Sir Guy know?' Johnson asked.

'He will. We ought to have got the warning through to him by this time.'

'And he's still going to ride out?' one of the other men asked. 'There's no chance of cancelling the Show?'

'Cancel the Lord Mayor's Show?' Lutterworth's voice was nearly as cold as his eyes. 'This may be the longest-running Show in the world. Five hundred years. It's the original Show that must go on. There was also an IRA bomb threat against it in 1974 – and the Show went on just the same.

'Do you think Sir Guy Carraway wants to be the first Lord Mayor to say, "Whoops, I'm windy – let's call the whole thing off, chaps"?'

'Do you think *we* want to be the first City of London Police to admit we can't police our own City?'

'Better get going, hadn't we?' Constable Johnson spoke into the silence, diverting attention from his tactless and unhappy colleague. 'Where are we picking up the procession?'

'They've already started.' Lutterworth checked his watch. 'So we'll catch up with them when they pause at Mansion House. We'll pack off the two civilian clowns already in Clover's party and go on from there. That way, we'll be accepted as part of the Show and no one will notice us.'

There was an uneasy laugh.

'I mean – ' Lutterworth corrected with a wry grin. 'No one will question our presence. Let's synchronize watches – '

They did so. The familiar gesture was somehow reassuring, even though time, as such, had little to do with the problem they were facing.

'Right – ' Lutterworth took a final look round and nodded. 'Let's go!'

'Good luck!' the make-up man said again, impartially, to all of them.

'We'll need it!' Lutterworth thought.

CHAPTER XI

Elaine was out there somewhere. *Elaine the fair, Elaine the lovable, Elaine the lily maid* –

Elaine had slipped away into the anonymous crowd – beyond recall. Elaine – with Timothy and Geraldine. *What, all my pretty chickens?*

Guy shook his head, trying to clear it of quotations, of sentiment – even of the terrible knowledge that had been so suddenly thrust upon him.

And so unwillingly, so incredulously, received. This was *his* day, the culmination of a lifetime of hard work – and good luck.

How could it have gone so wrong? How could his luck so inexplicably have deserted him?

Through the protective haze which engulfed him, he was aware that the police officer had left the room, that other men had now entered. Vaguely, he recognized them as City colleagues. Once they had been part of his life, his interests; now they seemed like creatures from another world.

Yet *he* was the one from another world – a world into which he had been abruptly returned. These people, worthy and valuable members of the community though they were, could not help him, could not even reach out to him. There was no point in discussing what had happened – what might happen – with them.

'We'll carry on as usual,' one of them said. The others murmured agreement. 'Can't let the crowd

down. Can't let some maniac think he can frighten
us into calling the whole thing off.'

Guy nodded. He had expected no less of them.
They were good men – and they would be in the
leading carriages, half a mile ahead of the presumed
target area. Ahead of him.

They moved down the stairs in a body, making
jokes with the familiar bravado of the beleaguered
facing battle. They had, in their own way, gone back
to their own war.

But they were an older generation – none of them
had been in *his* war. Guy watched them climbing
into carriages, giving V signs to each other, laughing,
determined not to treat the threat seriously – or
seem to. Putting their faith in the Authority which
had assured them that everything possible was being
done, that the madman would be captured before
doing any damage. Perhaps they even believed
the assurances.

Their war had been a cleaner, neater war, with
clear-cut objectives. Their war had also bred in
them a confidence in their structure of command,
in the reliability of their subordinates, in the bene-
volence of their God.

They had never had to stand alone.

Yet no one was quite alone. Barney hovered on
the outskirts of the official group, still cavorting
for the benefit of the kids, but waiting an opportunity to move forward for a final word before their
part of the procession moved off.

Guy caught Barney's eye and signalled. The years
fell away and he used their old signal from the
Korean days, swift, silent and urgent. He saw the
sudden change in Barney's face as the years fell

away for him, too.

'What's up, Lucky?' Barney was at his side, responding to the urgency, knowing that something had gone wrong somewhere – very wrong.

Guy told him.

'Christ – Jean!' Barney's thoughts flew to his own hostages to fortune. 'Jean and Little Jean – they're going to be watching from somewhere around St Paul's.'

'Get to them,' Guy ordered. 'Send them home. And if you see Elaine and the kids, send them packing, too!'

'Steady on,' Barney said. 'I can't go racing through the crowds in this get-up. I'm supposed to be following your coach. Everyone knows it. There's been publicity about it, and it's in the programme, too.'

'Forget the procession!' Guy said. 'And keep away from my coach! No one will think too much about it if we don't follow the programme exactly. You're on foot, and it's easy for the foot marchers to get too far ahead or too far behind. Drop out of the procession as we get to St Paul's – '

If we get to St Paul's.

The thought flashed between them. There was no way of knowing where the bomber might choose to strike. Even now, he might be in the crowd across the street, ready to hurl his missile as the Lord Mayor's coach moved into line in the procession.

'Tell you what I'll do,' Barney said. 'I'll send Young Guy off now. He's only carrying the spare pies and won't be missed. He's younger and faster than me – he'll go through the crowd like an eel.

He can find Jean and Little Jean. Elaine and the kids, too. Don't worry, Lucky, we'll get them out of harm's way.'

'You, too,' Guy said tightly. 'Did you hear me, Barney? I want you to keep clear of the coach.'

'I heard.' Barney looked at him levelly. 'You reckon you're the target, is that it, Lucky?'

'Keep clear of the coach,' Guy repeated. 'If you *have* to stay in the Show, why don't you move up with Clover and the clowns? You won't look out of place there. If anyone notices the switched position, they'll just think it was because we decided a nursery rhyme character fitted in better with the clowns.'

'Nice try, Lucky.' Barney shook his head. 'But I'm not buying it. I belong back here.'

'God damn it, Barney! Do as I say!'

'You don't give me orders these days.' Barney reached out and jingled the great chain of office around Guy's neck with amusement. 'You're in the wrong uniform for it, Lucky!'

'Barney –' Guy switched to pleading. 'Be sensible. What good will it do if both of us cop it? Who'll look after Jean and the kids, and Elaine and the kids?'

'My insurance is paid up – and I'll be surprised if yours isn't. Young Guy is shaping up like a dream. He's almost ready to come into the business anyway – a bit of extra responsibility won't hurt him. Speaking of which, I'd better talk to him and start him on his way.'

'Barney –' Guy's hand on his arm stopped him as he was about to turn away.

'Sir Guy – !' The summons came from a footman

who was holding open the door of the Lord Mayor's coach.

'Off you go, Lucky!' Behind the smile, Barney's face was shadowed, as though he, too, wondered what had happened to the bright and shining day this had promised to be.

'I wish you wouldn't, Barney.' Their hands came up and clasped each other's shoulders briefly, in a gesture from the old days before they set out on a mission.

'Take it easy, Lucky,' Barney said. 'This isn't the first minefield we've walked through together.' Unspoken, they saw the same thought mirrored in each other's eyes.

But it might be the last.

Sir Guy Carraway, Lord Mayor of London, waved a smiling acknowledgement to the cheers of the crowd, paused by the door for a photographer, and then boarded his golden coach.

CHAPTER XII

The crowd was not yet impatient. The smaller children were sitting along the curbstone on newspapers or folded cardigans their parents had put down for them, enjoying the preliminary spectacles of the day.

Mounted policemen grinned and waved to the sporadic cheers of the children as they rode past. Programme vendors, their sacks hanging limply now, were on their way back to base, shaking their heads regretfully at would-be customers. The flag and balloon sellers still had plenty of stocks in reserve; the programmes always sold out first.

Would a programme help? Hilary wasn't sure, but wished she could get one just the same. Perhaps she might spot a seller with just one left. If she were lucky . . .

Lucky! Hilary looked out over the crowd with a surge of despair. They were going to need more than luck – they were going to need a miracle.

'She's here. She's here *somewhere*.' Maureen O'Fahey pushed against the crowd, forcing open a pathway. She was met by an occasional muttered remark but, for the most part, even the most vehement shove brought only laughing protest. It was a very nice type of crowd, as Hilary had heard old-time constables nostalgically remark about former assignments.

'She might be on the other side of the street – '

Maureen turned a despairing face towards her – 'and we'd never know. Maybe you ought to take one side of the street and me the other.'

'It wouldn't help,' Hilary said gently. 'I don't know what she looks like.'

'Oh, God, you don't! You've never even seen her picture. And I – ' Maureen groped for a hanky. 'I don't even *have* a decent picture of her. If – if anything happens, I'll be left with nothing at all – '

'Steady,' Hilary said, as Maureen's perilous control began to slip. 'Everyone is doing everything they can. The worst won't happen. We won't allow it to.'

Maureen's sniff was comment enough on such a reckless promise. 'You *have* to say that,' she accused, but the idea of splitting up had been sidetracked.

'It's true.' Hilary hoped fervently that it was. Certainly the part about doing everything they could was true. Her experienced eye had noted the gradual increase in blue uniforms dotting the crowd. There would be others, like herself, in plain clothes.

For some time she had been conscious of the clatter of a helicopter overhead, swinging out to the perimeter of the crowd on either side of the parade route and then back again, quartering the area, slowly making its way down from Mansion House to the Royal Courts of Justice in the Strand where the procession would halt for the Lord Mayor to be presented and sworn in and, incidentally, for the officials to partake of lunch.

After lunch, the procession would resume its slow progress, turning down Arundel and Surrey Streets into the Victoria Embankment, and along the Embankment and Queen Victoria Street back to Mansion House where it would disband.

The whole procedure would take about three hours altogether. Three hours – with no way of guessing where or when the man with the bomb would decide to strike.

Would he want to make his sensation in the early part of the proceedings, perhaps hoping to catch the final edition of the evening paper? Or would he prefer to wait, hugging to himself the knowledge of what he was about to do, like a miser gloating over his gold?

And where? At the Bank of England, if he nursed a particular grievance against the economic policies of the country? Or perhaps at Mansion House itself, underlining his antipathy towards the pomp and majesty of the proceedings? They didn't know anything about him, that was the trouble.

Or Fleet Street? Right in front of one of the major newspaper offices? When the taxi had passed that way, Hilary had noticed that her colleagues were moving in that direction. Was that what the higher-ups were betting on? And were they right? Or had they been misled by their own sensitivity towards public relations, imagining that everyone was as conscious of publicity as they were?

Three hours. The longer the bomber delayed, the better chance they would have of apprehending him.

But, Hilary cast a professionally assessing glance over the girl beside her, could Maureen O'Fahey stand three hours of so intense a strain without cracking up?

Yes, Hilary decided, Maureen could stand it – on the "while there's life, there's hope" principle.

It was when there was no more hope that there would be serious trouble with Maureen O'Fahey.

CHAPTER XIII

It was too bad about the horses. That was all he really regretted. Those beautiful, curiously graceful Shire horses, annually loaned by Whitbread's, the City's oldest brewery, to pull the Lord Mayor's coach. Six glorious creatures to pull over four tons of golden carriage, plus the honourable lords inside, and creatures who always seemed to relish the occasion as much as any Alderman.

He'd try to figure some way around it, some way to spare them. They, after all, had nothing to do with the iniquities of Man. Like so many others, they were just victims. Creatures of circumstance, condemned to a role they could not comprehend.

But that was one thing he had to give the English – they looked after their horses. Even the cart horses pulling junk wagons were groomed and gleaming and stepped out jauntily, secure in the confidence that they were admired by every passer-by.

And the brewery horses were the cream of them all. Always beautifully groomed, today they'd look more special than ever, satin ribbons braided into their manes and tails, harnesses gleaming, they seemed to know their importance. Know it – and enjoy it. As they enjoyed the cheers of the children, the music of the bands, lifting their great, spreading, clod-hopping feet delicately, almost in time with the nearest band, the graceful fetlock fronds floating with the movement. Ah, they were God's finest creatures. It was going to be an awful waste. It was too bad about the horses.

'Da – ' The tiny, irritating hand tugged for his attention, the voice shrilled to a whine. 'Da, I'm tired. There's the parade. Can't we stop here and watch? I can't walk any more.'

'Oh, for – !' He bit down on his fury for fear of eavesdroppers.

'Come on now, Kitty,' he coaxed, forcing a smile. 'Just a little way farther. We want the best spot for you to see it all, don't we?'

'I'm tired,' she whimpered.

'Not much farther,' he pleaded, glancing around. As he had feared, they were attracting attention again. Those damned interfering faces, turning towards him, looking at him, perhaps remembering him. And Kitty.

No matter that, for the moment, those faces wore sympathetic smiles or grimaces of shared martyrdom. Later, someone might think again, remember, report to the police.

'Look – ' He looked around frantically, noting what others were doing. Already some of the children too tiny to plough through the crowds, too frail to be battered against the surge of strangers, were riding triumphantly aloft – borne on the shoulders of a father or uncle.

'Here, I tell you what we'll do – ' He swung her up to his shoulder. 'I'll give you a ride for a while. How will that be, eh? You like that, do you?'

'Whee, yes!' Kitty crowed triumphantly. 'Oh, I can see everything now!' More people turned to smile at them.

'All right, all right, easy now,' he placated. 'Keep a tight hold on your lunch box now. If you drop it – ' He caught his breath. 'If you drop it, we'll never find it again in all this crush.'

'I'll take care of it,' she assured him earnestly. He could sense her taking a tighter grip on the lunch box. She'd hold on for dear life now after that warning. She'd better.

'Oooh, look, Da! Look over there!' Now he could realize the extent of his mistake as she tugged at him again. This time, at his hair.

'Please, Kitty,' he said, between clenched teeth. 'Don't pull my hair. Don't pull poor Da's hair. You don't want to hurt him, do you?'

'No, no – ' The grip slackened, his scalp retracted, still smarting. 'But, look – ' Her voice shrilled upwards causing his eardrums to wince. 'Can't we stop here and watch?'

'Just a little farther,' he urged. At least, he was in complete control now that he no longer had to pace himself to her little steps. He kept moving.

'No!' The hand clenched on his hair again.

'We'll do it this way – ' he said hurriedly. 'We'll go just a little farther, and then we can see the whole parade go past on their way to Mansion House.' That way, he would be able to verify the programme and make certain there had been no last-minute changes. It would also let him check the accuracy of the programme timing.

'Then we'll nip down a short cut,' he went on, 'and we'll get ahead of the parade again. That way, we'll be able to see it all a second time – '

'We will?' She had stopped pulling his hair, enchanted by the prospect.

'That's right,' he said. 'All these others – ' he gestured towards those standing tightly-packed along the pavement. 'They'll only see it once. But *we're* going to see it twice!'

'Twice!' she exclaimed exultantly. '*We're* going to see it twice!'

'That's right. And furthermore – ' he promised recklessly. Anything to keep her quiet and content. 'If you're really good, maybe we can even see it a third time. They'll stop for lunch half-way. And we'll be able to get ahead of them *again* and watch them on the way back.'

'Again!' she sighed ecstatically. 'We'll see them *three* times!'

They wouldn't. There would be no fine expensive lunch for those buggers, no extension of the pomp and ceremonies they loved so well. There would be only the blast and the blood – retribution.

'Da – ' She twined the fingers of one hand in his hair thoughtfully, the stick of the flag gouged into his head. Her other arm circled his neck, the lunch box bumping against his chest. He gave a quick downward glance to make sure she retained a safe hold on it.

'Da, I'm hungry.'

'Oh – !' With an effort, he managed not to curse her. There was an ice-cream truck parked in a side turning ahead. 'You'll have to have an ice-cream then, won't you?' His voice rang hollow in his own ears, but it must have sounded all right to her. She responded with enthusiasm.

'Can I? A big one?'

'Yes, yes.' He pushed his way over to the truck. It was that damned sloppy kind, half-melted as it slid into the cone. But at least there wasn't a queue. It had been seduced away by the promise of movement down the street.

'A big one,' he ordered, passed it up to her, and moved away quickly before the ice-cream man had time to notice them – or before Kitty blurted out something that might make him mark them especially. That was the worst of her, you never could tell what she'd come out with next. Or what she might do. Were all kids like that?

He looked around him. Probably they were. He saw them, in all shapes and sizes, smiling, sulking, whining, wanting what they couldn't have, trying the patience of adults who had been kind enough to give up a Saturday to try to please them. Ungrateful brats, all of them, even the quiet ones – they were only biding their time before *they* raised hell. It would be a better world without them.

'You're going too fast!' The shriek nearly burst his eardrums. 'I'll fall off. I'll fall!'

'You won't fall.' He slowed down. 'Do you want to walk again then?'

'No!' He could feel the vehemence with which she shook her head. 'I just don't want you to go so fast.'

At first, he thought the icy chill at the back of his neck was just another manifestation of the rage he was trying so hard to control. Then he realized what it was as it spread and the stickiness adhered to his skin and began slithering down his back.

'Hold your ice-cream steady,' he snarled. 'You're dripping it down my neck.'

She laughed. Damn her! She laughed. At him!

'Oh, look! Over there! More clowns – over there!' Her hand, sticky and wet now, clutched at his hair once more, jerking his head upwards with each tug.

I'll kill her, he thought, *I'll kill her.*

Then a curious sense of peace and calm enveloped him as he realized that that was precisely what he *was* going to do. This very day. Her and as many others of these screaming, puling little brats as he could get in range.

It was a pity about the horses, though.

CHAPTER XIV

Donovan came up out of St Paul's Underground Station and stood quietly blinking in the misty light, only his eyes moving cautiously from side to side as he looked around. If anybody was noticing him, he must have looked a right shifty-eyed bastard, the sort who'd just run out of a police station while he was being questioned.

As, indeed, he had.

Had he asserted his rights as a free man and walked out on the police – or had he been allowed to leave? He'd have felt slightly more comfortable if he were certain of the answer to that one.

That was his trouble, he decided. Essentially, he was too law-abiding.

But it was not his own trouble he ought to be worrying about right now. It was poor little Maureen O'Fahey's trouble he had taken upon himself to try to help. Him and what looked like the entire police force of London and the Home Counties. And God help all of them!

He looked around again, moving his head this time. So far as he could determine, no one was aware that he was there at all. He might be the original Invisible Man.

Well, just so long as that kept up, he'd have no complaints. Evidently his face showed no signs of his terrible knowledge – thanks be to God. If any suggestion of the terrible scenes which had been playing themselves out across his imagination showed upon his face, surely the crowds would have recoiled in horror rather than walking calmly past him, unnoticing.

He'd come to St Paul's Underground Station because it seemed to him that it was important to be here. However, through not being familiar with the station, he'd come up the wrong exit and found himself on the far side of Cheapside, with the parade crowds blocking his way across the street.

Not that he had any real reason for this hunch about St Paul's Cathedral. He'd never heard Mike Carney make any comment about religion. Or about much of anything, bar the weather, the rise of prices, or the probable paternity of one of the more unpopular foremen.

As he'd tried to explain to the police, they hadn't been what you might call friends, at all. Just workmates – and devil take the day he'd suggested Mike might like the spare room at his digs.

If he hadn't, all this wouldn't be happening now.

Rather, he qualified the thought, it might be happening, but he wouldn't be aware of it. It would be happening to other people. It wouldn't be little Kitty O'Fahey, so trusting and innocent, some-where out there now with death in her tiny hands. And it wouldn't be poor little Maureen O'Fahey – no longer trusting, and a long time since she'd been innocent, poor girl – out there searching frantically now.

The thing was, he'd got them into it. Could he get them out of it? In one piece?

Could all the King's horses and all the King's men get them out of it? Or, more accurately, all the Lord Mayor's men?

Would the Lord Mayor himself be in one piece tonight after this Show had ended?

But – St Paul's? Why did he have St Paul's so firmly fixed in his mind?

Donovan thought back. No, he couldn't bring to mind any positive recollection of Carney's ever making any specific reference – good or bad – to St Paul's Cathedral. Was it, then, some reflection of an attitude towards church or clergy that he had caught?

Should he say something about it to the police?

No, he vetoed that idea instantly. They would only start asking him why he hadn't told them before. And it had only come to him once he was on his way. He always thought better when he was moving – action lubricated the brain cells, perhaps.

Also, they would demand to know where he was now. Precious time would be lost while they tried to argue him back to the station or into waiting where he was while they traced the call and sent someone to collect him.

No, he'd do better on his own. He could travel faster, and he could recognize Carney – even if he'd tried to disguise himself. He knew Kitty and, more importantly, Kitty knew him. With luck, she even trusted him. If he were to shout at her to run, she'd run and wonder why later. By then, even if she'd got lost in the crowds, they could find her again. And she'd be safe. Anywhere but with that one.

Cheapside was packed solid with people and kids – so many kids. The men and women were about equal in numbers and there seemed to be about

three kids for every one of them. A bomb bursting in the midst of this lot didn't bear thinking
about.

How could he have worked beside Mike Carney
for so long and not have noticed that the man was
warped to the point of madness? How could he have
talked to the man, and drunk with him, and
brought him under his own roof and not noticed?

It was no use saying nobody else had noticed it
either. *He* hadn't noticed it – and *he* had been the
one to introduce the man into his digs. Perhaps
others had sensed something wrong and veered
away.

So, why hadn't he?

There was a burst of music in the distance and
anticipation rippled the children like a wind. Faces
turned in the direction of the sound, flags began
waving, sporadic cheers broke out.

Oh, Christ! Donovan reeled back. One of the
faces ran with blood.

People looked at him curiously. '*Drunk* – ' he
could see the judgement form in their eyes – '*and
at this hour.*' The woman with the bloodied child
pulled it closer to her, away from the danger of
contact with him.

He got a final look before the child turned, and
his heart steadied down to a moderate hammering
again. Not blood. Just a deep pink skein of candy-
floss running from mouth to chin and unnoticed as
yet by the doting parent.

Not blood – this time.

But – next time? If he didn't find Carney –
next time? It didn't bear thinking about. All these
kids. Lambs to the slaughter.

The dirty maniac! Donovan looked around wildly. Somewhere in this crowd, somewhere along the winding route of the procession. Somewhere, Carney was lurking. Waiting. Deadly and treacherous as a poisonous snake concealed in the camouflaging foliage. Unsuspected by the innocents passing by.

With an effort, Donovan pulled himself together. Fury – no matter how righteous – wouldn't help. This wasn't a time for fury. Not yet. This was a time for cold calculation, for trying to fathom the workings of a mind that had taken leave of its humanity and was whirling through the outer regions beyond reason. How could any sane man hope to figure it out?

The day was darkening, storm clouds scudding through the sky as the wind rose. Rain before long, most likely. Although it had looked like this earlier this morning, only to clear. It might clear again.

Donovan lifted his head, his eyes drawn by the dome of St Paul's. Why did he have this feeling about it? Was it some kind of premonition? Or just a false lead?

The dome rose high and proud. Behind it, the storm clouds massed thick and dark, like clouds of billowing smoke. Like smoke . . . like that wartime photograph . . .

And then Donovan had it. The memory that had been tugging at the edges of his consciousness: the day he and Carney had paused outside a bookshop window on their way back from lunch. There had been a display of books about the Blitz and, naturally, that classic photograph had taken pride of place. And Mike Carney had stood there looking at it, with a curious expression on his face and just the hint of a smile sneaking around the corners of his mouth.

Had he been planning it as far back as that? It was after he had come to live at the lodgings, but before he'd ever said a word to Maureen O'Fahey – or to little Kitty.

Not much to go on, the expression on a face, but Donovan felt that he was right. That was what Carney, in his madness, planned. To destroy both the Lord Mayor of London and St Paul's Cathedral. Or as much of both – and as many people around – as he could with one bomb.

But . . . Donovan looked again at the great towering mass of the Cathedral. It would take more explosives than Carney could muster to make even a dent in that massive façade.

On the other hand, a bomb exploded anywhere in the vicinity of the Cathedral would surely envelop the dome in the billowing black clouds that had seemed to give Carney such satisfaction.

Of the target there could be no doubt: the Lord Mayor of London. And now Donovan was certain that the target area was St Paul's. The chief dignitary of the City was to be assassinated within sight of the landmark that had become the symbol of that City.

As the parade began to circle and move past the Cathedral, somewhere the attempt would be made. And he, Donovan, was the only one who had any suspicion of that fact at all.

Disregarding the protests of those around him,

Donovan began shouldering his way through the crowd, driven by a fresh sense of urgency. He had to get across the street before the parade reached this spot and held him immobilized.

He had to get to St Paul's.

CHAPTER XV

They were moving in fits and starts, and this was not due solely to the pressure of the crowd around them. Rather, it was because Maureen O'Fahey would suddenly come to a dead halt and turn around slowly, scrutinizing every child's face in sight as though, if she stared hard enough, one of them might turn into the face she wanted to see. Then, after what seemed an interminable time and sometimes brought a nervous murmur from the accompanying adult, she would plunge wildly back into the surging crowd and dash for what she imagined might be another vantage point. Hilary had all she could do to keep up with her.

'Wait a minute – ' Out of breath after the latest spurt during which she had nearly lost her, Hilary clutched at Maureen's coat. 'This isn't getting us anywhere. We ought to – '

'We can't stop!' Maureen pulled away, head turning ceaselessly, frantically. 'She might be anywhere. She might be at the very next corner!' Once more she sprinted forward.

The crowd grew thicker, impeding her progress. Hilary was able to keep half a pace behind her without too great an effort. Then Maureen halted again, so abruptly that Hilary bumped against her. She turned to Hilary urgently.

'What are they doing there?' she demanded, pointing to a pair of uniformed constables who were walking along on each side of the street, pausing every few yards to make a general announcement to the crowds along the curb. 'Are they telling them about Kitty? Are they asking them if they've seen her?'

'I don't know.' Hilary doubted it. This was not a situation where taking the general public into official confidence would do any good at the moment. Quite the reverse.

'Oh, let's get over there!' Impatiently, Maureen began pushing her way towards the curb.

They struggled curbward until halted by a waist-high wall of children. On the other side of the wall, a policeman halted in the gutter, addressing the adults over the heads of the children.

'Now, when you see the Lord Mayor's coach,' he said authoritatively but confidingly, 'you look around and get a sighting on your kiddies. Because that's just about the end of the procession and the crowd starts breaking up after that. You make sure you know where your kiddies are and get ready to catch hold of them. Remember – ' he began walking along, repeating the warning to those farther along the curb – 'When you see the Lord Mayor's coach – '

'It's nothing.' Maureen turned away in despair. 'Nothing!' She began pushing through the crowd again to the single-file footpath still open at the back of the pavement. She hesitated as she reached the clearing, then turned in the wrong direction.

'We've come that way.' Hilary caught her and gently turned her in the opposite direction. 'They aren't up there. If we keep following the route, just ahead of the parade, we'll have the best chance of catching up with them.'

'Yes. Yes, I suppose you're right.' Still, Maureen hesitated, her glance turning backwards. 'But how do we know they aren't back there now? How do we know we haven't missed them?'

'We didn't see them,' Hilary said firmly. 'And we looked as well as we could. I don't think we could have missed them.'

'But how do we know they haven't got round behind us? Maybe they stopped somewhere else first. Maybe they're just getting there now – and we're ahead of them.'

'*They're* ahead of *us*,' Hilary said. 'They wouldn't be behind us, even if they'd just arrived. The parade has already started up there. They'd miss it and – '

'And they wouldn't want *that!*' Maureen finished the thought, somewhat wildly. 'You're right. We've got to go on. They'll be ahead of us somewhere.' Without waiting for a reply, she lurched forward again.

Hilary plunged after her, caught once again by surprise. It was the way Maureen seemed to surface from her preoccupation, speaking almost rationally, that threw one off guard, Hilary decided. But Maureen was tiring visibly, she had been swaying with fatigue during that last exchange. When had the girl last eaten?

Catching up with her, Hilary put the question.

'Eaten?' Maureen looked at her vaguely. 'Eaten? I don't know. Who can stop for food at a time like this?' Her eyes turned away, searching, the question already forgotten. 'Where *are* they? Oh, where can they be?'

'They're still ahead of us,' Hilary said reassuringly, taking a firm grip on her arm. 'There's plenty of time yet. We can stop somewhere and have coffee and a bun.'

'No!' Maureen tried to pull away from her. It had been the wrong thing to say. 'There's no time. No time at all!'

'Very well, then,' Hilary soothed. Ahead of them was St Paul's Shopping Precinct, with the myriad coffee houses and luncheon counters of Cathedral Place and Paternoster Square. Once there, she could surely entice Maureen inside one of them for a few minutes – even if they had to gulp something standing up. Without sustenance, Maureen could not keep going, and it might be necessary for her to endure for hours more.

There were anticipatory noises along the street and the rustle of children stirring and straining to see the first signs of the approaching parade.

'Come on,' Hilary tried to urge Maureen through the narrow gap that would let them get across to the other side of the street. But they were too late. The crowd ahead of them shifted and blocked their way. A pair of mounted policemen cantered past, followed by a slow-rolling armoured vehicle. There were a few shouts from the children along the curb, unsure whether these developments augured the real parade or were just another false alarm.

Then the first of the brass bands marched into view. The drum major surveyed his waiting audience with a grin, sure of his power. He brought his baton up, shouted a command to the band behind him, and swung down the baton. The music rollicked out and along the street:

'*Seventy-six trombones*
Caught the morning sun . . .'
The cheers of the children drowned out the noise
of the helicopter hovering overhead.

CHAPTER XVI

Try not to think about it, as the coach rolls along. Acknowledge the cheers of the crowd. Smile at them, wave to them, look as though you're enjoying yourself. This is the culmination of your career, isn't it? Sir Guy Carraway, Lord Mayor of London – the man sitting on top of the world.

Until someone blasts him off.

Keep smiling, keep waving. It was the inability to do anything personally about it, the inactivity, that was so nerve-racking.

The other men in the carriage cleared their throats and shifted restlessly, unwilling to speak until he had given them some conversational lead. He watched their eyes as they nervously tried to assess the crowds, but his own eyes slid away every time one of them attempted to meet his gaze. He wasn't ready for conversation. How could he be, when there was really nothing to say.

Either they'd make it or they wouldn't. It was as simple as that. No amount of discussion would change it.

Keep smiling. Keep waving. The cheers broke out afresh every few feet as the coach jounced along. They were both a greeting and a thank-you for the parade that had gone before. Many of the children were waving tokens which would entitle them to groceries, pies, or a television programme attendance. Even the ones without tokens seemed happy and cheerful, undoubtedly realizing that a few judicious tears later would make up their loss.

Keep smiling . . . keep waving . . .

Where was Elaine? He hadn't seen her yet along the route.

'*We'll dodge in and out of the crowds along the way,*' she had said. '*We ought to be able to see you at a dozen places . . .*' and '*How many children can ever have memories like that?*'

Not many. Not his, he hoped. Not if the memories were to include those of seeing their father blown to smithereens before their eyes.

But, if they were close enough to see that, they'd be in danger, too. Worse, if the bomb were badly aimed, if the wayward effects of blast were to take them and leave him –

Keep smiling . . . keep waving . . .

He was suddenly sharply aware of Barney, prancing just opposite the window now, keeping pace with the coach, like an outrider. Barney, giving him the thumbs-up sign but, when their eyes met, forced to shake his head regretfully. They hadn't found Elaine and the kids yet.

Elaine and the kids. And how many other kids? It took an effort of will to unclench his fists, to let his hand fall in the easy wave of acknowledgement the crowd expected as they roared their thanks for the spectacle he had presented for their entertainment today.

Their entertainment . . .

He glanced upwards, losing that train of thought. All those people on the rooftops, crowding upper storey windows of the buildings along the route. Of course, the police had thought of them, were keeping watch as best they would. But how much good would that do? They couldn't cover every roof, every window. Would they even see a small parcel falling in descending arc aimed straight at the golden bull's-eye of the coach roof? And, if they saw it, what could they do about it?

Keep smiling . . . keep waving . . .

This was what Royalty went through all the time. Well, perhaps not quite all the time, but often enough. Once was too often. The small and lonely targets, going about their business with every outward show of confidence, trusting to security forces who were necessarily composed of fallible men hoping to hell they could avert the threat. Hoping it was from an obvious nut they could spot before he did any damage, hoping it was just a bluff. And, being human, hoping that if anything did have to happen, it would happen on a day when they personally were off duty and at some spot miles away.

The coach slowed and lurched to a halt by the wooden steps leading up to the grandstand at Mansion House. Someone in livery rushed forward and opened the coach door. It was time to mount the grandstand and take the salute.

Would it happen now?

The spattering of applause broke out from the people in the grandstand as he started up the steps. He scarcely heard it. He raised his head, knowing the smile was safely frozen on his face and saw the answering, welcoming smiles on the faces that watched his progress. Not one of them the face he really wanted to see.

Elaine should have been here. But she had been so firmly set on the idea of taking the children out amongst the crowds on such a great day that he had indulged her. There would be other days, other occasions, other grandstands . . . he had thought.

As from a great distance, he heard people talking to him. From a greater distance, voice travelling down a wind tunnel, he mouthed responses. They must have seemed adequate, although he was un-aware of what he was saying, for the faces remained unmoved, still smiling, still pleasant, still happy to share his moment of glory with him.

Hands patting him on the shoulder, hands push-ing him forward to the front of the grandstand, hands pattering together in the endless applause again. They meant well. They didn't know, they couldn't know, the truth of the occasion, the taste of ashes in his mouth.

He was at the railing now, in the centre of the throng of dignitaries and honoured guests. His lips still twitched in response to the pleasantries being bandied about on all sides. Only the whiteness of his knuckles as he grasped the railing in front of him might have betrayed his state of mind – if anyone had been noticing such a minor thing.

He stared out over the crowd – it was thicker here than at any point thus far along the route. So many faces, so many blurred, so many hidden behind taller people. Was Elaine out there with the children? If they were standing there watching him being honoured, would it be the last thing they would ever see?

A silence fell over them all, the hush of waiting for something to begin. There was a strange whirring undercurrent of sound – the noise of hundreds of cine-cameras recording the scene as part of a record of tourist holidays abroad, or a home movie of holidays and events, sandwiched between Bank Holiday at Bournemouth and Grandma's Golden Wedding. Absently he remembered the amateur film of the Kennedy assassination and wondered if there would be some lucky survivor out there in the crowd who would unwittingly record the whole event and find that his hobby had paid off in world sales of faultily focused footage which had accidentally captured an historic event. The death of the Lord Mayor of London on his inauguration day. The Lord Mayor – and how many others?

The Show must go on. In the distance, he was aware of the massed procession stirring and shuffling in preliminaries to the march-past about to start.

Beyond them and above them, he saw the first ray of hope. Not a ray, but a darkening, lowering of the cloud cover, bringing the threat – no, the promise – of rain.

Rain. Rain could save the day. Especially a lashing torrential downpour that would break up the crowds and send everyone scurrying for home. Even a lighter misting rain would set anxious parents worrying about colds and sniffles and pulling their little ones away from the front line, back towards the shelter of the buildings along the way, into doorways, towards something that might resemble safety. Rain might save some of them.

Sir Guy Carraway raised his face to the blackening sky. '*Let it rain*,' he prayed silently. '*Let it pour. Let it come down in sheets and torrents . . .*'

The procession in the distance began to move forward. He kept smiling.

Let it rain . . .

CHAPTER XVII

If it rained, it would be even better.

Mike Carney looked skywards, measuring the chances. The clouds had melded together into a dark solid overcast which was growing darker by the moment.

Good.

He craned his neck to look over the heads in front of him. Nothing happening. The long, final pause before the whole thing swung into its proper form and marched past the Lord Mayor when, after most of it had passed, he would descend the steps, get into his coach once more and take his place at the end of the procession – the high point of the parade. Oh, it would be high, all right!

'Da – ' The brat was whining again. 'Da, I can't *see*. I can't see anything.'

'There's nothing to see,' he snapped. 'They're just all standing around waiting like the rest of us.'

'Let me see. I want to see.' She smiled winningly. 'Lift me up again, just for a minute, so I can see.'

'Later.' He never should have put her on his shoulder in the first place. She'd learned a new trick now. 'You're heavy.' His shoulder still had a numb ache where she'd been sitting so long.

'Please, Da – ' She tugged impatiently at his hand. '*Please.*'

'We're moving on in a minute,' he said. 'Just keep still, there's a good girl, while I see – '

'But I want to see, too.' She would not be quiet.

She was attracting attention again, her voice had risen and was carrying through the crowd.

'Shhh, all right.' He caught her up briefly, swinging her up to allow her a brief glimpse and lowering her to the ground again. 'I told you there was nothing to see.'

'Yes, there was. I saw lots of things. Just let me look again. Just a little look. *Please*.'

'We're moving on now.' Get her out of the way before the first band began playing, before she realized that something was going on. It would be harder to move her, once the parade had started. She wouldn't want to give up the procession passing by for the promise of a better look at it farther along.

'Come on.' He pulled gently, wishing he could jerk her off her feet and see her stumble to her knees, then drag her through the crowd. But he couldn't, not with the little packet she was carrying.

'I'm tired.' She began moving reluctantly. 'I'm awfully tired, Da. I can't walk any more.'

'Just a little way,' he coaxed. 'It isn't far, and it will be downhill most of the way.'

Downhill. Across and around behind St Paul's, then down Ludgate Hill. To the crowds standing under the railway bridge at the foot of Ludgate Hill.

If it rained, it would be even better. More and more of them would crowd into the enclosed space, seeking the shelter of the overhead bridge. An explosion there would not only take care of His Precious Lordship, but would destroy the railway bridge and disrupt suburban train services, whilst the effects of the blast in that small enclosed area would be more violent than at any other point along the route.

The foot of Ludgate Hill, it would be.

'Da – ' She was tugging at him again, impeding his progress. 'Da, I've got to tell you something. Da – stop and *listen* to me!'

'All right.' He stopped, not trying to disguise the frown on his face. 'What is it?'

'Don't shout.' Unexpectedly, she hung her head and half turned away. 'I can't tell you if you shout at me.'

'All right.' He controlled his voice carefully, forcing a more pleasant expression on to his face. 'All right, I'm not mad at you. I'm just impatient, see? I want to get to the best spot before it's too late. Now, tell me, what's the matter?'

'I want – ' She turned to him, turned away again. 'I want to go.'

'Go?' He stared down at her dumbfounded. 'But we haven't been here all that long. You haven't seen the parade yet.' If she went, if she tried to run away, it would ruin everything. 'You can't want to go home now.'

'I don't want to go *home*,' she protested, with a flash of irritation at his obtuseness. 'I want to *go*.'

'Go where?' He continued looking down at her blankly. What was she talking about?

'*Go*.' The sudden, convulsive twist of her body ended his doubt. 'You know, *go*.'

Oh, Christ! He'd never thought of that. All his plans had depended on never letting her out of his sight once they had reached the parade route. And now this.

'Can't you wait?' he asked hopelessly. 'It won't

be much longer now.'

'I can't wait,' she wailed urgently. 'I have to *go*.'

'Oh, Christ!' he muttered. What was he going to do? He couldn't take her into a Gents with him, and he couldn't go into a Ladies with her.

'Hurry.' She had begun squirming graphically, attracting amused looks from bystanders. Damn them! And damn her, too!

'All right.' He began striding forward, she had to half run to keep up. 'If you want to go, then come on.'

There were public lavatories in the buildings at the corners of Paternoster Square. It would mean letting her go down alone and hovering at the head of the steps like a fool until she came back up again, but, if they hurried, there was time, and she would attract far less attention than dancing around the way she was now.

'I'm hurrying, Da.' She gave a little running skip to try to match his stride.

'Don't jump around so,' he gritted, between clenched teeth. He kept his eyes fixed on the goal ahead, marked by the dome of St Paul's. He couldn't look down at her – if he did, he couldn't trust himself not to strike her. If it were possible, he'd abandon her this instant, leaving her lost and alone, not knowing how to get home . . .

Ah, but she'd pay in another way for all the annoyance she was causing him. He looked around at the smiling, laughing faces of the crowd.

They'd all pay.

CHAPTER XVIII

'*You owe me five farthings . . .*'

'*When will you pay me?
When will you pay me . . .?*'

'*When I grow rich,
When I grow rich,
When I grow rich . . .*'

The great bells of the City rang out their carillons in joyous welcome to the new Lord Mayor of London. The melodic clamour overrode all lesser sounds, drowning out the cheers of the crowd, the clatter of the helicopter, the music of the bands.

'What's all that?' Maureen O'Fahey jumped nervously. 'What's happened?'

'Nothing,' Hilary soothed. 'It's just the start of the Lord Mayor's taking the salute. It's all right.'

'All right . . .?' Maureen O'Fahey echoed, lifting her head, listening, waiting.

Hilary, caught, suddenly lifted *her* head, listening too. The bells continued to ring out, no sound more disturbing interrupting their melody.

She had not been aware that she was holding her breath until the sudden choking feeling made her gulp in air quickly. *One more dangerous moment past.* The feeling was so strong that she nearly voiced it, remembering just in time that, to Maureen O'Fahey, every moment was potentially dangerous. It would be of little import to her to realize that the police had feared an attack at the start of the salute. It would be of no comfort to her that, after all, the explosion of bells had not masked a deadlier explosion.

The next most likely target now was the Royal Courts of Justice in the Strand, where the procession would stop for the Lord Mayor to be presented, and to have lunch. There would be the bustle and confusion attendant upon parking carriages, dismounting, walking on foot through the courtyard. The dignitaries would all be out in clear view – and within easy hurling distance of a bomb – both before and after the ceremonies and lunch in the Courts. Hilary knew that, as soon as the Lord Mayor had left the grandstand at Mansion House and taken his place in the parade once more, most of the guards at Mansion House would hurry along to reinforce those already at the Royal Courts of Justice.

'Oh, come!' Maureen O'Fahey was moving forward again. Hilary dismissed the brief idea of taking a short cut to the Royal Courts of Justice. Maureen would never stand for it. They were obviously doomed to plod along every foot of the route, however hopeless it might be. It gave Maureen O'Fahey the illusion that she was doing something and, without that illusion, she could not get through the hours ahead.

Nor was she likely to get through them if she didn't stop for sustenance. She was looking around with that desperate anxiousness again, but swaying on her feet. She couldn't last much longer.

'This way,' Hilary said firmly, leading her behind the crowd to Panyer Alley Steps.

'No – ' Maureen held back. 'The people . . . everyone . . . they're over *that* way.'

'Nothing will happen at the moment,' Hilary said. 'The Lord Mayor is still at Mansion House. He's too well guarded there. Nothing can happen until he rejoins the parade.'

'But Kitty's here somewhere – ' Maureen tried to twist away from the hand grasping her arm. 'Kitty – '

'I know,' Hilary said. 'And, believe me, we're looking for her. All of us. She'll be found, she'll be safe. But you must come and have a cup of coffee now.'

'No – !' Maureen broke free and stood there, almost dazed. 'We've got to keep looking.'

'Well, *I* need a cup of coffee.' Hilary gambled. 'It will only take a couple of minutes – ' She began to turn away, not looking at the other girl.

The steps were wide and shallow, she moved forward slowly and put her foot on the bottom step. Nothing happened. She had to ascend that step, and the next, and then another. She had lost. Maureen O'Fahey would disappear into the crowds and they would never catch up with each other again. And what might Maureen do, running frantically through the crowds? If she were to begin speaking to any of the public, telling her story, starting a panic . . .

'All right!' Suddenly, desperately, her arm was caught from behind. 'All right!' Half-sobbing, Maureen O'Fahey was at her side again. 'But, for God's sake – hurry!'

The clamour of the bells drowned out Hilary's involuntary sigh of relief.

'Bells, bells, bells, bells,
Bells, bells, bells . . .'

Hilary bit down on an incipient hysteria she had not realized was so close, and smiled reassuringly through the renewed noise at Maureen. Uncertainly, Maureen smiled back.

They were going to stay together now, that much was assured. The danger that Maureen might break away from her and disappear into the crowds had passed. A dependency had been established, however tenuously. If Maureen had been alone from the beginning, she could have borne to be on her own now. But, having had someone else to talk to, to exchange glances with, to worry with, to cling to, she could not bring herself to face being on her own. She would allow Hilary a cup of coffee, she would even indulge her to the point of taking one herself, if Hilary insisted.

'Nearly there,' Hilary encouraged. 'It won't take any time at all, and we'll both feel *so* much better.'

Maureen made a choked sound that was not quite a laugh.

'This way – ' Hilary abandoned any thought of trying to retrieve that last remark. Practically anything one said could turn out awkwardly at a time like this. They were at the top of the Steps now and she led the way along the passage to Cathedral Place.

Maureen followed docilely, her head still turning to scan every face they passed.

'In here – ' It was a coffee bar that was not too crowded and they could have a table by themselves. The service would undoubtedly be quick, as the waitresses would attend to them so that they would vacate their table rapidly in time to accommodate the high tide of patrons who would flood in after the parade had passed.

'Oh, wait!' At the door, Maureen pulled back. 'Can't we just stand here another minute? Just another minute?' Desperately, she searched the passing faces.

Ahead, in Paternoster Square, a fun fair had been set up. Electronic music vied with the bells, and the throb of portable electric generators powering the carousel and train rides pulsed with a beat of its own, underscoring the music. Occasional shrieks of children's laughter rose above the noise, but not many. It was too early yet. After the parade had passed, the fun fair would come into its own and receive the crowds.

'She ought to be down there – ' Maureen appealed to Hilary. 'Kitty ought to be down there, begging to go on the rides, the way she does. Having a good time, not – '

'I know,' Hilary said. 'I know.'

'Oh, God!' Maureen was close to tears again.

'Come inside.' Hilary urged her into the coffee bar gently. 'The sooner we have our coffee, the sooner we can begin hunting for her again. Don't worry, we'll find her.'

'*When will that be* . . .?' the bells mocked. '*When will that be* . . .?'

The coffee bar door swung shut behind them, muffling the melodic rejoinder.

'*I do not know,*
I do not know,
I do not know . . .'

CHAPTER XIX

They came up the stairs at the corner of Paternoster Square and began walking towards the Ladies lavatory. It was too much to hope that she wouldn't notice the fun fair.

'Oh-h-h!' Her eyes widened with delight, she moved forward eagerly.

'Over here.' He held her back. 'You wanted the Ladies, didn't you?' he reminded her. 'That's over here.'

'Oh-h-h . . .' She twisted in both directions almost simultaneously. 'Oh, I want to go on the rides.'

'Later!' He ground his teeth. She had half the adults in the vicinity looking at them again, smiling, trying to catch his eye. How had he ever got the idea that he'd be more inconspicuous with a kid in tow? And it was too late to abandon her and make other plans now.

'But I haven't been on any rides for ages, Da.' Her lip quivered. 'Not since my birthday. My mother always lets me. My mother – '

'Your mother isn't here now!' He didn't want her to start thinking along that tack. Who knew what else she might say? What she might let slip?

'I want my mother – ' Tears filled her eyes. 'You're not nice! You're hurting my hand! I want my mother – '

'You want the Ladies Room, too,' he said quickly, trying to distract those around them more than her.

'And here it is.'

It was down a flight of stairs. There was a bend at the foot of the stairs, which meant that she would be out of sight once she was down there. He wouldn't know whether she had to queue, whether she'd set her little lunch box down on the floor, or whether she might try to balance it on the edge of a slippery sink while she washed her hands. Suppose she took it into her head to open it and peek at the 'surprise' inside – ?

'Let me hold your lunch box for you while you go down there,' he said casually, his teeth on edge, fresh perspiration trickling down his forehead at the thought he tried to suppress. 'And your flag. It will be easier for you to manage then.'

'No.' She swung them away from him, balky, obstinate, asking for a good clip across the ear – but too many witnesses around for him to give it to her.

Christ! 'Come on, now,' he coaxed. 'You can keep the flag, but just let me take the lunch box then. It might be dirty down there. You wouldn't want to get it all dirty, would you?'

'No!' Her chin jutted out, she looked at him suspiciously. He had given it to her, now he was trying to take it away again.

'You can have it back,' he said. 'I'll just hold it for you while you're down there, like. Directly you come up, I'll give it back.'

'No!' She began her painful contortions again. 'Let me go. I want to *go* now!'

'Ah, God!' Still he clung to her, looking around desperately. Dare he snatch it away from her? He'd like to – *and* send her on her way down the stairs with a kick. But the witnesses, the witnesses.

'I'll take the little girl down for you.' Some interfering busybody of a woman was at his elbow, smiling at what she imagined to be his dilemma. 'My daughter and I are just going down ourselves.' She transferred her smile to the children at her own side. 'And those look like the stairs for you over on the far side of the Square, Timothy.'

He hated her. He hated her accent. He hated her presumption. He even hated her pretty face. What business had she to interfere?

'You'll come along with me, won't you?' She extended a hand to Kitty. And Kitty reached out to take it, with the hand still holding her lunch box.

'That's kind of you,' he said, quickly fawning, sensing an opportunity. 'You go along with the nice lady, Kitty, and I'll be waiting right here for you, don't you worry.' He looked at the woman with a conspiratorial wink. 'And you'll let me hold your lunch box while you're gone, won't you? It will be easier for you to manage without it.'

'That will be much better,' the woman said, becoming an ally. 'We won't be long – Kitty, is it? Let your father hold your lunch box – '

'He's not my – '

'This is very kind of you.' Hastily, loudly, he drowned out the beginning of Kitty's protest. 'Go along with the nice lady now, Kitty. And, if you hurry,' he added craftily, 'you'll have time for one of the rides before the parade comes by. Just one, mind – ' Should he say anything to the woman about, perhaps, being an uncle or a friend of the family? Explain, in case Kitty decided to set the record straight once she and the strangers were out of earshot? No, perhaps not. Perhaps Kitty, distracted by the promise of a ride, had already forgotten what she had been going to say.

'You promise?' Kitty was going to nail him down in front of these unexpected, but welcome, witnesses.

'I promise.' Over her head, he smiled at the woman again. The woman returned his smile, with just a trace of impatience.

'But just one, remember.' Gently he detached Kitty's fingers from the handle of the lunch box, still talking smoothly, keeping her attention firmly focused on the future rather than on what he was doing. 'After the parade has gone past, we can come back here and you can go on the other rides.'

'All of them?' she demanded.

'All of them,' he promised recklessly. 'We'll have the whole afternoon in front of us. You can go on all the rides you want.' He watched her face begin to glow, her eyes dance. There'd be no more trouble there. 'Just hurry along with the lady, lovey, and don't keep her waiting. She wants to see the parade, too.'

'I certainly do.' The woman smiled warmly at him. 'So, come along, Kitty. Come, Geraldine – ' With a final smile directed at him, she took each of the girls by the hand and began descending the stairs.

Mike Carney watched them go. Just as they neared the foot of the stairs, he saw Kitty lift her head and say something to the woman. He started forward, but they turned the corner and were out of sight – and he was left standing with one foot on the stairs plainly marked 'Ladies' and likely to attract that deadly amused attention again.

He reared back quickly and moved off the stairs. It was too late now. There was nothing he could do. He leaned against the wall in sudden weakness.

What was happening down there? What had Kitty said to the woman? He should never have let her go down there. But what else could he have done? If Kitty told the woman the truth –

But Kitty didn't know the truth. And how damning was the bit she could tell? Only that he wasn't her father – just a friendly neighbour who had taken her to the parade. Surely every kid here today couldn't be with a relative – some of them must be with friends.

The woman had smiled at him and seemed to approve of him. Could her opinion be reversed by anything Kitty might tell her? Surely not. He found himself beginning to breathe normally again.

There was nothing suspicious in anything he had done so far. Even taking the lunch box had seemed perfectly natural – the woman hadn't raised an eyebrow. It was just a thoughtful gesture on his part. And, without the lunch box, there was no evidence.

Besides, even if the woman's suspicions were aroused, what would she actually *do* about it? The English were great for minding their own business. Anyway, she was shut away down there now and he'd see her if she tried to get past him – with or without Kitty – and get to a policeman.

They didn't have telephones down in those places, did they?

He heard a faint rattling noise and, tracing the source of the sound, found that his hands had developed a fine tremor which was jiggling the handle of the lunch box in its little metal loops. Jiggling the lunch box, as well. With a concentrated effort of will, he stilled his hands. It was only a little while longer now. Just a little while.

But what, in the name of God, might Kitty be saying to the strange woman – the unknown quantity – down those stairs?

CHAPTER XX

The Lord Mayor had returned to his coach and resumed his place in the procession. The Company of Pikemen and Musketeers of the Honourable Artillery Company, who were supposed to follow behind him as escort, had been moved farther back and a police car had quietly taken their place.

Thanks to other quiet reshuffling of the order of march, Lutterworth and his policemen-clowns were escorting Clover the Clown just in advance of the Lord Mayor's coach. Too close, really, for the orderly progression of a normal parade. The cheers for one group would not have time to die away before fresh cheers were raised for the Lord Mayor. It would all jumble together and become indistinguishable. In the ordinary way, most unsatisfactory for both parties.

But the public wouldn't notice, that was the important thing. They'd simply assume that the order of march had got a bit muddled, if they thought about it at all. They were in holiday mood and wouldn't worry if their printed programmes were not precisely accurate. Most of them were too busy juggling kids to be able to look at their programmes, anyway.

There had been another minor reshuffle, as well, and the Lord Mayor now rode alone in his golden coach. Sir Guy had insisted – and the police had backed him. It would be easier if he were alone. His colleagues had made the expected perfunctory protest, and then given in with a fair amount of grace. Perhaps the ride from Gresham Street to Manor House had been enough for them, really bringing home to them what they would be up against during the long slow procession through the City.

Sir Guy Carraway rode alone. But the Pieman still cavorted close by the side of his coach, Lutterworth noted. Simple Simon seemed to have disappeared, however. Not so simple, after all.

There was quite a wide gap between the Clover contingent and the Lord Mayor's coach, where an intervening military band had been removed and slotted into a different place in the procession. With luck, that empty space might give them room to manoeuvre.

If they reached a position where manoeuvring might do any good, that would be luck in itself.

The policemen-clowns were spread out along both sides of the street, handing out the four-leaf clover tokens to the kids along the way – which allowed them to get a good look at the crowds behind the kids. It was as well that the paint on their faces. distracted attention from the sharp searching eyes quickly scanning each sector of the crowd as they passed.

Clover the Clown pedalled his pennyfarthing down the centre of the road, occasionally veering to left or right, as though the machine were fighting him for control – to the delighted screams of the children.

Lutterworth was not so delighted. Why couldn't the clown see what he was doing? Every time he veered toward the kids, they surged forward,

reaching out to try to touch him, calling to him –
shifting the formation of the crowd, in fact. And
each minor disturbance might provide a screen for
Carney to act behind.

But Clover seemed to take no joy in the delight
of his audience. Perhaps the amount of make-up on
his own face allowed Lutterworth to see beyond
the mask of greasepaint on Clover's, where every
lineament was set and taut. Without the concealing
make-up, he would look like a man on the verge of
cracking up. Was he?

Certainly, Clover knew more than most about
what was happening. It had been necessary to
confide in him when they impinged on – rearranged
– his whole personal appearance in the parade.
He had co-operated. Willingly, it had seemed.
And yet . . .

Clover worried him. Lutterworth admitted it to
himself. There was something about the clown's
behaviour that was not quite right. It was funny,
yes. It was erratic, okay. But it went just slightly
beyond the bounds of clowning – even clowning
in the face of danger and uneasy knowledge. There
was something too erratic about it.

Smiling to the crowds and waving his hand to
the children who shrieked with delight as he nearly
tripped trying to avoid an equine souvenir directly
in his path, Lutterworth kept his main attention
focused on Clover. Let the others search the crowds.
Right now, it was Clover who was the source of
some new, unspecified danger.

In the last few moments, Lutterworth had become
convinced of it. Unobtrusively, he speeded up his

pace, moving closer to the clown.

Clover bent his head and concentrated on pedalling just as fast and furiously as he was able to. The pennyfarthing lurched forward, trick gears engaging, and ricocheted towards the children on the left-hand pavement, then those on the right. They whooped with exhilaration, urging him onwards.

The fools. The poor bloody little fools. They didn't know. They had no way of knowing . . .

He pulled up abruptly, taking the pennyfarthing back into the centre of the road, trying to steer a straight course. For how much farther? How many more miles? Past how many thousands more laughing, trusting, childish faces?

Clover inadvertently met the steely gaze of the Ringmaster – that was the way he thought of him – and looked away quickly. Even after all these years, it took a definite effort at times to remember that *he* was the star attraction now, the Chief Clown. That is, he *had* been. But not here, not now. He had been superseded by that strange interloper in the ill-fitting costume, who was as patently in command as though he were in top hat and tails, flourishing a Ringmaster's bullwhip and signalling the acts into the centre ring.

The pennyfarthing veered towards the right-hand pavement again and the children standing there cheered and reached out to him, imploring him to descend from the old-fashioned machine and come and play with them.

So trusting, that was the bit that killed him. That might so easily kill *them.* Surrounded by loving relatives, watching a beloved idol perform, their

God was in his heaven, all was right with their world. What could they know or suspect of the darker forces that lay beneath the surface?

Of its own volition, the pennyfarthing seemed to sway towards the laughing groups of children. One moment they were looking up at him, each face bright and clear; the next moment they were face-less blurs. He knew the tears were in his own eyes, still hidden from the watching children. If they noticed his tears, they would laugh harder than ever, because that was the funniest thing of all – a clown crying. That was the funniest thing he could do, wasn't it?

That was why the great clowns were the sad clowns, why the lines on their faces were all painted downwards, why the eyes turned upwards, the mouths drooped. It was the perennial joke between clowns and children – they cried, too. And for the same reasons, the same silly, nonsensical causes: they couldn't tie their shoelaces properly; their puppy wouldn't jump through a hoop at their command; essentially, because they couldn't com-mand the world around them. Not and be obeyed.

The pennyfarthing wouldn't go where he wanted it to go. He wrestled the steering bar with exagger-ated fury, automatically playing for the laughs he could hear but no longer see.

Another clown had wept in real life once. Captured in a prize-winning photograph for all the world to see. A triumph for the photographer, a voyeuristic thrill for the public, but a nightmare that had seared into Clover's young brain as the ultimate horror a performer could face.

The great Emmett Kelly – tears coursing un-

ashamedly down his face – at the Hartford, Connecticut, circus fire. Emmett Kelly, with the pathetic
little bucket that had been part of his act filled with
water, rushing to throw that tiny splash of wetness
against the blazing inferno of canvas that had
engulfed the audience of children who had been
brought to the circus as their holiday treat. All he
could do. While the firemen battled with hoses and
water supplies that could never be adequate to the
catastrophe that had suddenly been unleashed on
the holiday crowds; while the children who had
been laughing happily a few minutes before were
now shrieking with horror in the smoke and flames.

All he could do. One tiny bucket that had held
less moisture than the tears flowing from him. All
he could do to try to help the children who adored
him, and whom he loved in return. Not much.
Not nearly enough. But all he could do. While the
tears flooded across his make-up, acknowledging
his impotency, his uselessness, his inability to be of
any real help when the chips were inexorably
down.

Poor Emmett Kelly. Poor, poor Clover.

And poor, poor, poor children – helpless innocents. Victims to be sacrificed in some mad adult
game of politics, insanity and revenge. Who could
save them? Who could help them? Who could
even explain to them when their torn mangled
bodies lay stretched out in hospital beds facing the
months and years ahead when other adults tried
to put them together again – tried to make them
understand why this had happened to them in the
first place?

They had been in the wrong place at the wrong

time – the antithesis to the classic recipe for success. But why? How did you explain that to them? How did you make them understand that? Why them? Of all the children in the world, why them, at this time and in this place?

To see Clover, that was why.

Clover shook his head – it didn't help, neither clearing his mind nor dispersing the blur from his vision. Only his ears remained unaffected, the sound of childish high-pitched laughter a benison, and a reproach.

'Run! Run!' He pedalled straight at the nearest children, his voice a faint thread of sound against the laughter and the cheers. 'Run away! Save yourselves!'

The laughter swelled and grew into a roaring overwhelming sound. They didn't believe him. They thought he was trying to be funny again.

'Run away!' Blinded by his tears, he could no longer tell where the pennyfarthing was steering. 'Listen to me! Save yourselves!' The laughter drowned out his voice.

'Listen to me! Believe me – ' A bleak cold despair settled over him. He remembered the plight of a silent screen comedienne attempting her first serious part. In the midst of a harrowing deathbed scene, the audience had started laughing. The more agony and pathos the actress had poured into the scene, the more the audience had howled with merriment. It was then that studios and performers had begun to realize the mysterious power that subsequently became known as type-casting. Once a comedian, always a comedian. The public refused to recognize you otherwise.

The pennyfarthing veered across the road, towards the other side where the laughter was not so loud. They might hear him better over there. They might listen.

'Run – ' he shouted. Abandoning the steering bar, he waved his arms at them wildly, trying to shoo them away.

'Save yourselves! Run for your lives – '

The Ringmaster was suddenly at his side, shouldering the large front wheel back towards the centre of the road, even at the risk of tipping the pennyfarthing over.

'That's enough of that,' Lutterworth said severely. 'What are you trying to do – start a panic?'

Clover fought for balance, the machine tilting perilously, the old half-forgotten fear of falling from a great height reasserting itself. The fear of the pennyfarthing tilting and hurling him to the earth.

The scolding was still going on. He deserved it. The Ringmaster was right. Starting a panic would do no good. Even getting rid of one little cluster of children would do no good. His small bucket of water was useless – he couldn't save them all. He couldn't save any of them.

'Sorry.' The machine back under control, he looked down at the policeman. 'I'm all right now. It won't happen again.'

The policeman nodded briefly and moved away – but not too far away. Clover was miserably aware that he was going to be under close surveillance for the remainder of the day. He had achieved nothing but the destruction of his own credibility. He was no longer to be trusted.

Worse, he was now an additional burden on his

escort. He knew that the crisis was past – that he would not crack up again – but they didn't. For the remainder of the procession their attention would be divided between the crowd and keeping a wary eye on him.

Clover raised his head to look at the children he had just tried to wave away. Tears blurred his eyes again.

They were all laughing and waving back at him.

CHAPTER XXI

Donovan was swimming against the current. As the
last two police cars crawling in the wake of the
procession passed, the crowd broke ranks. From
both pavements, they flooded out into the middle of
the street, heading, as though with the determination of a single mind, for the purlieus of Fleet
Street and of Blackfriars, where they might find
restaurants and snack bars in which to snatch a
hurried lunch en route to their homes or into the
West End for an afternoon of shopping.

Behind them, they left the City, already shaking
the last of them free of her trailing skirts and pre-
paring to sink back into her usual Saturday slumber.
Ahead of them . . .

Donovan hoped that most of them were going
straight home or to the West End stores. Nothing
had happened so far – and they wouldn't know how
lucky they had been until they turned on the television tonight or read tomorrow's newspapers and
found out what had happened to the poor devils
who had elected to watch the parade farther along
the way.

If everyone was truly lucky, of course, there'd
be no news at all. That mad Mike Carney would be
safely intercepted and put away where he'd menace
innocent people no longer.

Not that he, Donovan, would have anything to
do with it. Not if he didn't box cleverer than this.
Buffeted by the onrushing tide, he was still only

half-way across Cheapside – and the devil of a way to go yet to reach St Paul's, for all that it looked so near. The procession had taken the dog's leg down behind the Cathedral, whence it would proceed along the Cannon Street·side and emerge at the top of Ludgate Hill. He wanted to be there before they reached that point, before the Lord Mayor's coach got to the front of the Cathedral.

Donovan began shouldering his way across the oncoming crowd with increasing urgency. He *had* to reach the other side of the street quickly, *had* to get to the Cathedral before –

'Watch it, mate!' The shout halted him and as soon as he stopped moving, he lost ground again, carried along down the street with the crowd.

'Sorry – ' He apologized uselessly to the man whose child he had nearly knocked over. Both man and child had been swept away in the flowing mass.

But the moments gained had been lost, and he struggled to free himself from the pinioning swarms around him. With the use of some blunt language and pointed elbows, he succeeded in breaking free of the mainstream and fought his way to the opposite curb. Even there, it wasn't much better.

There was a solid unyielding bottleneck trying to get down the steps to St Paul's Underground Station. They presented as immovable an aspect as St Paul's itself. It was not a time or a place for anyone in a hurry. Most of the crowd weren't. The kids were treating it as just another part of the day's adventure, even the adults were laughing and exchanging remarks with the good humour that had been in evidence all morning.

Donovan faced the human bulwark hopelessly

for a moment, then abandoned the idea of trying
to get through. He walked farther along Newgate
Street to one of the sets of anonymous steps that led
up into Paternoster Square. He could cut across
Paternoster Square, go down Paternoster Steps,
and come out in front of St Paul's. He had hoped
to be able to cut across the back way, past Panyer
Alley Steps and down New Change to catch up with
the parade before it reached the Cathedral.

Too late for that now. Even though the procession was proceeding at a snail's pace – no doubt
slowed down by official request in order to give the
police more time to attempt to vet the crowds
along the way – it would still be past before he
could get to the point where he had planned to meet
it. So, in front of St Paul's it would have to be. And
pray God that nothing happened before they reached
there.

He reached the steps he was looking for and found
he wasn't going to have an easy passage here, either.
The crowd was flooding up the steps all around him,
threatening to knock him off his feet, sweeping
him along with them as they began fighting their
way through to the fun fair in Paternoster Square.

Some of them, obviously, were going to try to
catch up with the parade for another look. Others,
equally obviously, had finished with that for the
day, forgotten it already, and were intent on the
rides, the food stalls, and the tents where they might
win a doll or souvenir by their prowess at some game.

He wished them luck. Nice for some people that
that was all they had to worry about.

'Hurry, Timothy – ' He heard a pleasant-
looking fair-haired woman say. 'We've been waiting

for you. We want to see Daddy again, don't we?
What kept you?'

'There was a queue,' the boy replied. 'Let's
hurry.'

They were already lost to sight, swirled away in
the moving flow of the crowd. People with someone
marching in the parade – God help them. God
help them all.

Donovan moved purposefully towards Paternoster Steps and St Paul's Churchyard at the foot
of them. It was back into the fray, down there. The
parade had not yet reached this point, but he could
hear band music moving in this direction. The
crowd was solid and murmurous with expectation,
heads turning towards the source of the music.

Two ambulances were parked by the statue of
Queen Victoria just behind the crowd and their
drivers and attendants were huddled together,
apparently more interested in having a cigarette
than in the oncoming spectacle. Or was it just that
they were snatching what might be their last
moment of peace and normalcy before the world
exploded?

Donovan cursed under his breath. A largely
impersonal curse, directed at a world gone mad, a
section of humanity which would equate terrorism
and slaughter with patriotism – and always, oh
Christ! – always, a God who paid no attention.

He directed a shorter, more fervent curse directly
at the head of Mike Carney. May he rot in hell! –
and may he waste no further time getting there!

But alone. Not taking any innocent victims along
with him.

Donovan lifted his eyes to the towering dome of

St Paul's. His gaze was imploring, half fearful that he should see the sight he feared. Despite the fact that there had been no explosion – none that he had heard. They say you never hear the one that gets you, don't they?

But the dome was intact. Intact and eternal against the cold grey sky. A sky that seemed to darken more even as he looked at it.

He became aware that the fine mist was thickening. Without any more warning, the first heavy drips splatted against his upturned face.

Rain, by God! And wasn't that just all they bloody well needed right this minute?

Below him, the crowd shifted uneasily, but stood their ground, implacable in their determination not to be driven away just as the parade reached them. After all, it might be a false alarm, just a few drops and the worst of the shower might hold off until after the procession had passed. They could not give up their places now.

Still muttering imprecations, Donovan dived for Paternoster Steps. He vaguely realized that people were moving uneasily aside, nervously pulling their children out of his path. *Another drunken Irishman*: he could see it written all over their faces.

Well, better they should think that than that they should know the truth of the matter.

He was nearly to the top of the Steps when, out of the corner of his eye, he caught a glimpse of red hair and a sweet familiar face. He stopped in his tracks and whirled about, trying to reverse his progress, even as she moved away in the crowd.

'Wait a minute!' he shouted, pushing his way towards her. 'Stay where you are! Wait for me!'

CHAPTER XXII

What worried him was that he hadn't realized she was there until he felt the sudden frightening tug at the little red lunch box. Yet he'd swear he'd been on guard every moment, watching the stairs from the Ladies lavatory like a cat at a mousehole. He'd even been half-crouched, muscles tensed, he found as he straightened up and all the stiffened bones protested.

'*Here* I am, Da.' She was beaming up at him expectantly.

'So you are.' He was still rattled. Had he been so totally submerged in the last-minute checking out of his plans that he had been oblivious of everything around him? If so, who else might be creeping up on him?

'You promised,' Kitty was repeating. 'You *promised* – ' She prised at his fingers, trying to loosen his grip and regain her precious lunch box. 'You *promised* I could go on one of the rides!'

Had he? Probably he had. He'd have promised anything to shut that nagging little mouth for a few minutes. But time was running short.

'Don't you want to see the parade?'

'It isn't *here* yet!' She was close to tears of frustration, unable to free her lunch box from his grasp and now sensing that the promised ride was about to elude her. 'Just one, you said. You *promised*.'

'All right. All right.' He saw now how he had missed her. The woman and child she had gone into

the lavatory with were just coming up the stairs
now. He'd unconsciously been watching for the
three of them, rather than one small anonymous
child alone, looking like half of the other kids milling
around today. Well, that just proved how right he
was, didn't it? Who was going to notice one more
kid today? Feeling cheered, he loosened his fingers
and released the lunch box to her – gradually, so
that she wouldn't drop it.

'Oh, good, she found you.' The woman smiled as
she passed them. 'She got away from me downstairs,
I'm afraid. She's like a blob of quicksilver.'

'She is that,' he agreed quickly, then wished he
hadn't spoken. The expression sounded too Irish –
would she remember it later? Give evidence?
Identify him?

What if she did? He'd be well out of the country
before anyone thought to start looking for him. If
they ever did. He hadn't left all that many tracks
and there was nothing unusual about an Irishman
on a building site just walking off without notice.

Everybody got more upset when a child disappeared, though. He eyed Kitty thoughtfully.
She was gloating over her lunch box, enjoying
possession of it again. If he didn't distract her, she
might try to open it.

'One ride,' he said firmly. 'Which one will it
be?' He nodded dismissively to the woman who,
with her little girl, was already moving off, down to
the opposite corner to collect her little boy. No,
she'd never remember an encounter in a crowd
on a day like this. By the time she got home tonight,
she'd have forgotten it completely.

'That one over there – ' Kitty pointed. 'The one

with all the horses. The roundabout.'

'All right.' He let her lead him across Paternoster Square, stepping carefully over the network of power cables that lay like sated boa constrictors across every pathway. Portable generators throbbed from caravans parked along the edges of the Square, drowning out all lighter noises with a tireless pulsating insistence.

Would they even be able to hear the music of the brass bands signalling the approach of the procession above all this other racket?

'Ooooh – look!' They were words he had learned to dread. He turned his eyes in the direction she indicated, abruptly aware that the brat had been tugging him towards the carousel by a circuitous route. She had marked *this* destination first and had led him to it. 'What's that, Da?'

'It's an ox. An ox on a spit.' The men at the booth were beaming at her wide-eyed wonder. 'They're roasting an ox.' He couldn't hit her without witnesses now who looked as though they might interfere.

'What are they going to *do* with it?' She was playing up to the audience now, she knew damned well that meat wasn't roasted just for the hell of it.

'They're going to sell it.' He had to answer, trying to project a fond smile. 'They're going to sell roast ox sandwiches.'

'Can *I* have one?' Her eyes went even wider, cajoling, excited. 'Can I please, Da?'

'Later.' He fell back on the familiar promise with relief. 'It isn't ready yet. See that sign?' How well could she read? 'It says they'll start serving some time between one o'clock and two o'clock. It won't be cooked before then.'

'Well – ' she would not be diverted – 'can I have some *then*? Can we come back and have some then?'

'All right.' His smile widened, becoming more genuine – also more private. By two o'clock, not many people were going to have much of an appetite. Those interfering bastards were going to be left with a lot of roast ox on their hands. And might it choke them!

'What time is it now?' Having wrested the pledge from him, Kitty was restless for further concessions, more ambitious conquests. Her gaze was already roving beyond the spitted ox to the games of chance, the rides – even, praise be, to the patch of St Paul's Churchyard visible at the foot of Paternoster Steps.

'Nearly quarter past twelve – ' He tried to instil a sense of urgency. 'Nearly time for the procession to be coming along this way. We'd best hurry.'

'All right.' Unconsciously, she mimicked his attitude. 'But you said I could go on the roundabout first. You *promised*.'

'I remember.' The false smile beamed out at the watching concessionaires, bore down on her. 'But hurry along now. It looks like they're just about ready to start a ride going now.'

It was true. Several restless children sat astride the painted horses with varying expressions of impatience. The ride was not nearly full, nor could it be with most of its prospective customers still waiting for the parade. The man in charge had nearly stopped stalling, he needed only one more face-saving fare before he started the carousel revolving. Kitty provided it.

'Right!' The man swung Kitty up on a polka-

dotted steed. "Old tight, now. 'E-e-ere we go!'
Kitty's shriek of delight was drowned in the sudden
blare of nursery-rhyme music as the roundabout
took wings.

Glumly, Mike paid out the requisite charge and
watched her. He should have retrieved the lunch
box again, held it while she took her amusement.
Suppose she were to drop it? What then?

It had seemed such a good plan when he had
first worked on it. The trouble was that he had not
allowed for the vagaries of another, totally different
personality. He had not thought of her as an indivi-
dual at all. She was just a kid. How could he have
realized that she had so strong an individuality,
one so determined to assert itself?

Already, wisps of telltale red hair were escaping
the confines of the yellow sou'wester, shrieking for
attention. No, the plan hadn't been as good as he'd
supposed. But it was the only plan he had, and it
was too late to change it now. Clenching his teeth,
he waited for the ride to end. But he clung to the
persona he had chosen for himself: devoted Da.
He smiled through clenched teeth at her every time
she whirled past, he even remembered to wave.

Finally, the carousel began to slow. Kitty slid
reluctantly from her perch, watching him carefully
for signs of weakness. He'd only said she could go
on one of the rides – he hadn't said how *many* times
she could go on it. But his face was shuttered against
her and she recognized defeat.

'Thank you, Da.' She opted for charm, looking
up at him confidingly. 'That was very nice.'

'Come on, now.' He caught her arm roughly.
'We've wasted enough time.'

'Yes, Da,' she said demurely. She wriggled her arm a bit and, without his being quite sure how it happened, was hand in hand with him again.

Quicksilver, just like the lady said. She might just as easily have pulled free entirely and slipped away into the crowd. Yet he'd been certain he'd been holding her so tightly she couldn't move unless he deliberately allowed her to. Unconsciously, he tightened his grip.

'Don't, Da.' She wriggled again. 'That hurts!' Her voice rose in protest and heads turned to look at them.

'I just don't want you to get lost,' he said, for the benefit of the onlookers. He did not loosen his grip.

'Let me go.' She was playing up to the audience again, twisting and pulling. 'I don't like you any more. I want my mother!'

'Your mother stayed home today – and I wish to God I'd had that much sense!' He, too, was playing to the audience now and the guise of exasperated parent obviously rang bells. He found he was collecting sympathetic glances. For a moment, he warmed and wanted to expand his role – then remembered that he shouldn't be attracting attention at all.

'Come on!' He pulled at her sharply enough to get her moving, but not sharply enough to give any credence to her pose of being bullied. He had to get away from those prying eyes.

'Come over here.' Diverting her had worked before and it was working again. She followed the direction of his pointing finger and her face brightened.

It hadn't made up its mind whether it was a 'Try Your Luck' or 'Test Your Skill' stall; signs invited customers to do both. But it was the targets that caught Mike's fancy. Masked burglars tiptoed across the back of the stall, pursued by painted policemen, their eyes big as saucers. In fact, their eyes were saucers. White, fragile, tempting targets. Three balls for ten pence – and you could knock their eyes out.

'Can I try it, Da? Can I?' Kitty bounced with excitement.

'You couldn't throw that far. This one's for grown-ups.' He glanced down at her and came to a decision. There was time – just barely time. And you might call it a practice run, to get his throwing arm into condition again. He picked her up and swung her up on the counter.

'Just sit there quietly,' he said. 'And watch.' He put down a tenpenny piece and glanced at her severely. 'And don't wriggle around like that or the man will make you get down.'

'All right, Da.' She was instantly, improbably, still, her earlier fractiousness forgotten. He was back in command again and the small victory pleased him, as though it were an omen of the victories to come.

She watched him as he picked up the balls, weighed them carefully, then transferred one to his right hand and took aim. The lunch box was larger, a different shape but, mentally, it was in his hand and the burglar's left eye was the window of the Lord Mayor's coach. The Lord Mayor of London! He let fly.

There was a satisfactory crash and the burglar

was abruptly one-eyed. Kitty gasped with delight.
'You did it, Da. You did it!' she cheered.
He acknowledged her applause with a short nod,
grimly concentrating on the other eye. The Lord-
Bloody-Mayor!
'You did it again!'
Too intent to pay any more attention to her, he
aimed and threw the final ball – straight at the
policeman. Interfering bastard, like the rest of
them!
'Great! That's the stuff!' The stall holder drowned
out Kitty's cheer; a winner was the best loss leader,
it brought others clustering around anxious to prove
their skill, to gain the applause. Already people were
edging towards the stall. 'You win a prize, but – '
He set three more balls down on the counter en-
ticingly. 'Another three hits and you get a *bigger*
prize. Come on, 'ave a go!'
'No!' Abruptly, Mike backed away. Once again,
too many people were crowding around, staring
at him, watching him. 'That's enough!' He swept
Kitty off the counter.
'Your prize – !' The cry halted him. 'Don't forget
your prize.' Sod the prize! But it would be even more
noticeable if he refused it. Reluctantly, he turned
back.
'Now, what will it be? You're sure – ' the stall
holder nudged the balls a little nearer the edge of
the counter – 'you wouldn't like to try just another
tenpence?'
'No time!' he snapped, then tried to soften it.
'I brought the kiddie in to see the parade, you
know. And there, it's going past down Ludgate
Hill already.'

'We've seen that part – ' After an anxious look towards the street, Kitty relaxed. 'We saw it over there. I remember the tank.'

So did he. He wasn't altogether reluctant to delay just a bit longer, until the big military units passed out of sight.

'Maybe we can come back later,' Kitty said. 'We're coming back to eat some ox,' she confided to the stall holder. 'Maybe we can come here again.'

'That's fine.' Other customers were gathering and he was not so concerned about letting them go. 'Going to let the little lady choose, are you?' he prompted Mike.

'Yes. Right. What do you want?' Mike asked.

'Anything on the bottom two shelves,' the stall holder indicated them as though bestowing largesse beyond price.

'Hurry up!' Mike ordered. There was a band passing now and he was growing impatient again.

'I'll take – ' She hesitated over the choice before her, longing to spend more time, luxuriating in the final decision.

'Hurry up!'

'*That* one!' She pointed to a small plastic piggy bank, in the same bright red as her lunch box.

As she reached up to take it, her arm brushed against her sou'wester, knocking it askew. For a moment, the bush of bright copper hair was in full view.

'Be careful!' Mike jammed the sou'wester back on her head evenly, hiding the hair again. 'Watch what you're doing!' But it was what other people were watching that counted. Had anyone noticed? 'Come on, now.'

'When we come back – ' She was superbly confident, clutching her new prize. 'Will you win me some more? Will you win me that doll up there?'

'All right. Yes.' Promise her anything. 'Of course, I will.'

'Oh, lovely.' She sighed with contentment and looked up trustingly at him. 'You're wonderful, Da.'

CHAPTER XXIII

A target is the loneliest thing in the world. It exists only to be aimed at, shot at, destroyed.

Sir Guy Carraway glanced through the window as the coach rounded a corner. They were passing behind and around St Paul's Cathedral now, coming into the paved street lined with shops, curiously called St Paul's Churchyard. It probably had been the Churchyard once, possibly the burial ground, in the days when the City could afford such extravagances.

Outside, Barney moved closer to the coach, looked inside and shook his head before moving off to release another flutter of blackbirds to the excited youngsters nearby.

They hadn't found Elaine and the children yet.

Ahead of the coach, glimpsed occasionally over the backs of the horses, Clover the Clown lurched his pennyfarthing on an erratic course pursued by the comic policemen, who were not nearly so comic to anyone in the know. Evidently, they hadn't spotted anyone yet, either.

Then an unguarded expression on Barney's face suddenly made Guy realize how selfish he was to worry only about Elaine. They hadn't found Jean and Little Jean either.

Yet Barney was giving *him* the thumbs-up sign through the window.

Guy nodded to Barney and looked beyond him to the crowds. Silly to think he might be able to spot anyone from this moving coach, but the attempt gave him something to centre his mind on. Something beyond the bomb lying in wait.

He'd come so far. If it were to end now, he'd still had a good run for his money.

But not if he had to take others with him when he went. Not if it produced another slaughter of the innocents.

He shuddered involuntarily as he remembered how firmly they had dedicated this day to children, planning items that would especially appeal to them, aiming publicity at persuading parents to bring their children into town for the day. Give the kids a treat!

Would St Paul's Churchyard shortly see bodies laid out in it once again?

The pointlessness of it enraged him. Perhaps he owed the Almighty a death. Perhaps he'd been living on borrowed time since that Korean minefield. But what had these others done? Especially the children – their lives had hardly begun. They didn't owe anyone anything – not yet. Not for decades yet.

The cheers erupted afresh on both sides every time the coach moved forward a few feet into new territory. Guy waved mechanically, smiling.

Flags waving, bells chiming, everyone cheering. The day he had looked forward to. The day he had done so much to earn. The day that was dust and ashes.

Barney moved over to the coach again. He pulled a face and shook his head at the hopeful lift of Guy's eyebrows. *Just checking*, he pantomimed.

Checking what? The danger was outside. But

Guy nodded and smiled reassuringly. At least, it seemed to reassure Barney. Why should it? What magic talisman was another man's confidence? A feigned confidence, at that.

But, of course, Barney knew that. A target has no confidence. It can't be expected to have.

Barney, too, was feigning. Pretending that Guy's calm reassurance was calming and reassuring him, when it was impossible for anyone to be calmed or reassured in a situation like this.

For a moment, a genuine smile lit Guy's face. They were both a couple of con artists.

Barney grinned back, then his smile snapped off and he turned back to the crowd, obviously afraid he might miss something vital if he let his attention wander for too long.

Guy stopped smiling, too. In the instant before Barney turned away, a strangely fatalistic expression had shadowed his face. Guy recalled abruptly that Barney had been directly behind him going through that minefield, the second man in line.

Did Barney, too, feel that a long-standing debt was about to be collected? Had Barney also had the feeling that he was living – and prospering – on borrowed time? And that time had now run out?

A sudden flurry at the edge of the crowd caught his attention. He leaned forward to see what was happening. A disturbance – just what the police had warned them to look out for. Something out of the ordinary. Something –

He could see it now. It was a banner. It reared and dipped, then reared again, straightening itself so that its message blazoned out clearly.

'THREE CHEERS FOR LUCKY.'
As the coach drew abreast of the banner, the
'Hip-hips' began. Three cheers for Lucky.
Lucky Guy.
Dead Lucky.

CHAPTER XXIV

That copper hair was unmistakable. Donovan battled his way towards it, intent upon reaching the beacon which had blazed so briefly before being lost to sight. She was somewhere just ahead of him.

For a moment, he thought he'd lost her. Then the flare of fiery hair reappeared. He pushed his way towards her.

'Maureen!' he shouted. 'Maureen!'

Both girls halted. Maureen stared around her wildly, hearing the voice yet unable to see the source of it.

'Over here!' Hilary called. The crowd parted amiably to let him through.

'What is it?' As he came up to them, Maureen greeted him with a hope it hadn't occurred to him he might raise. 'Have they found her? Is there news?'

He shook his head, not able to disappoint her in words. 'I've come to help you look,' he said. 'We'll find her.'

'Oh!' The disappointment bowed her head, made her sway against him. He found that his arm was waiting for her, had already stretched out to steady her. It confirmed something that he had been suspecting for some time now, but hadn't quite been ready to face. In his waking hours, he successfully evaded it, but it crept through the dark passages of his brain in the depths of night, invading his dreams, signalling to him a truth that he refused to acknowledge during the light of day.

'I'm sorry.' Maureen raised her head. She was not going to break down – yet. She clung to the social niceties as to a life-raft. 'Pat, this is Hilary. Hilary – Pat.' Her head dipped momentarily again.

Hilary and Pat Donovan nodded to each other across her bowed head. Their mutual concern prohibited any inconsequential murmurings.

'Are you all right?' Pat asked Maureen.

'She's all right,' Hilary said at the same moment. 'We were just going down the Steps. We thought it would be the best place to . . .' her voice faltered. 'To catch up with the parade. And then, perhaps, to walk along with it . . .'

To Fleet Street. He nodded grimly, following the thought. It had been lurking at the back of his own mind, second only to the dark intuition about St Paul's. Whenever it happened – either now, or on the return journey – it would happen near the centre of world communications. So that news could be flashed quickly to every corner of the world. Publicity was the name of the game – of every terrorist game. A shepherd getting his throat cut in the empty wastes of some distant desert might be just as terrified, but he wouldn't make the headlines. And headlines were what Carney and his sort were after. Donovan wondered sometimes what would happen if the headline were to be denied them, the publicity turned off.

'I'm all right.' Maureen raised her head. 'Let's not stand about. Let's get moving, keep looking – ' Her voice broke.

One on each side of her, they moved off. Down Paternoster Steps, into the maelstrom swirling

behind the stationary crowd watching a Scottish
band, bagpipes keening, march past.

'Alas, my love, you do me wrong,
To cast me off discourteously . . .'

Two ambulances were parked in front of the
Cathedral. Donovan shuddered, trying to rein in
his imagination. They might never be needed.
With luck, and by the grace of God, they might
never be needed. (If God hadn't washed His hands
of the whole shooting-match of them a long time
ago.)

On the far side of ambulances and statue, the
band came to one of those halts which must seem
so inexplicable to the crowd today. Marking time,
kilts swaying, they kept playing.

'For Greensleeves was my desire . . .'

From somewhere farther down Ludgate Hill, a
whistle sounded. The band moved forward again,
piping themselves out of the scene.

'And who, but my Lady Greensleeves . . .'

In their wake, tumbled the clowns. The Chief
Clown – some sort of television celebrity – was
pedalling around in circles on his pennyfarthing,
surrounded by the others. Now and again, he waved
urgently at the children along the way and they
waved back with equal intensity.

The children. Donovan knew this sick feeling in
the pit of his stomach might remain with him for the
rest of his life if the worst come to the worst today.
It would knot his guts until the day he died,
whenever he saw a kid about the age of the kids
along the way. And, if it took him this way – without
any child of his own imperilled – what must Maureen
be feeling?

He looked down at her anxiously. She was white as a sheet – whiter than a lot of sheets he'd had in English lodging houses. She was oblivious of him, or of the girl with her, as she kept searching the crowd for the one face she wanted to see. The face she must see, if her own life were ever to have any meaning again.

'We'll find her.' Donovan took Maureen's arm, hoping he wasn't as great a liar as he feared. 'It's a long day ahead of us, after all. The parade's hardly started yet. There's miles they've got to go – '

He broke off abruptly, made aware by a flicker of Hilary's eyes that he was not being altogether comforting. The unfairness of it suddenly irritated him. He sent back a glare challenging her to think of anything that could be of comfort in a situation like this.

Unheeding, Maureen pushed ahead, fighting her way towards the curb where the smaller children were packed solid. Her head turned ceaselessly, partly searching, partly shaking a denial of the whole nightmare which had overtaken her. No child she could recognize was in sight. No Kitty. No hope.

Behind her, Donovan's chest swelled with a useless infusion of adrenalin. But there was nowhere to run; no one to fight. His heart thundered pointlessly. There was nothing he could do. The surge of energy had to be fought down, controlled, ignored. There might come a time when it would be needed, but that time was not yet.

And it might never be needed. He had to face that fact, too. Whatever was going to happen might already be happening some distance ahead, too far for them ever to catch up with it. There was a faint humming in his ears which came, he knew, from straining them to hear the sound he feared. Once the dull hollow boom of a blast reached them, it would be too late for any of them to be of any use. Too late for little Kitty. Perhaps too late for Maureen, as well. Would any more be left of her than of Kitty if that final blast were to sound?

Maureen swept one final despairing glance along the row of children at the curb and swerved away again. She was vaguely aware that hands reached out on both sides to steady her, but she brushed them aside. There was no time to bother with people, however well-meaning. They were of as little moment to her as the large drops of rain which were beginning to batter against her with increasing intensity. She would soon be drenched. What of it?

Hilary realized that she should have brought her umbrella with her when she started out that morning. It was a belated realization many people were sharing. They began calling uneasily to their children, all of whom seemed to have developed diplomatic deafness, refusing to be budged from their vantage points just as the main attractions of the parade were approaching.

Those with children firmly in hand were more mobile and herded together towards the shelter provided by the overhanging entrance of Juxon House just below St Paul's and, farther ahead still, the protection provided by the railway bridge at the foot of Ludgate Hill.

The marchers, like the children, seemed unconscious of the change in the weather. Bright smiles still proclaimed that this was the brightest of all possible bright days.

The women were watching for the child, Donovan decided, and that was natural enough. So, what he ought to be doing was setting his sights higher. About three feet higher. And looking for the face of the concealed madman he had been working alongside all these unsuspecting months.

A grown man would be harder to disguise than a child. That was why Carney had taken the child – to provide himself with a cover. It stood to reason that he wasn't going to leave the child instantly recognizable. At the very least, he must have provided some change of clothing for her. Unless he was such a megalomaniac that he thought the child's absence and his part in it would never be noticed. That could not be ruled out. But it was safer to assume that he had some awareness that he was not entirely infallible and had tried to make arrangements accordingly.

He'd have to change her appearance in some way. It wouldn't take much. One or two small changes for one small needle-child thrown into this haystack of children. Her own mother wouldn't –

Maureen started forward, eyes fixed on a late-coming child who was trying to slip through to the front. Halted momentarily in her progress, the child turned a laughing coffee-coloured face beneath dim ginger hair to laugh at a parent urging her on from the background. Maureen moaned faintly and fell back.

'Come on,' Hilary caught her arm. 'Let's cut down the back way – '

'No!' Maureen turned to Donovan for support. 'No! We *must* stay with the crowd.'

'That's right.' Feeling a traitor to both sides, Donovan answered her plea. What difference could it make? 'It will be better that way.' Would it? Who could tell?

Hilary's glance asked him that and he had to shrug in bleak despair. Who could tell anything? All he knew was that it was better to humour Maureen rather than try to force her on to a path she did not wish to tread.

It could well be too late already for poor little Kitty. They might be miles from the scene of action designated by Carney's disordered mind.

Maureen was all they had – and she was not beyond helping. Not yet.

'Oh, well.' Something of his thoughts must have got through to Hilary. In her turn, she shrugged. 'What do you want to do then?' She studied Maureen with concern, noting new lines which seemed to have appeared on the girl's face during the short time they had been associated. 'Where do you want to go?'

Maureen looked at her blankly, suddenly bewildered at having to make a decision.

'This way!' Donovan pulled both of them into the shelter of the Juxon House overhang. 'That's better, isn't it? You won't get so wet.' The sight of Maureen's pale face twisted emotions he had not known he possessed.

'Why don't we take a break for a few minutes?' he suggested. 'Why don't we have a cup of coffee?'

'We've just *had* a cup of coffee,' Maureen wailed. Her voice was at breaking point.

'Yes – ' Hilary looked out at the slanting rain. 'But I couldn't make her eat anything. She ought to. If you could – '

They both looked at Maureen and realized the hopelessness of even attempting this.

'All right, love.' Donovan took Maureen's hand gently. 'Where do you want us to go?'

'Down there – ' Maureen gestured along the parade route, towards the foot of Ludgate Hill. 'Down there – '

'Right you are.' He tucked her hand under his arm. 'That's where we'll go, then.'

CHAPTER XXV

They'd posted guards on top of the railway bridge. On top. That was funny. That was a real laugh, that was.

There were two policemen, prancing up and down, nice and inconspicuous in their fluorescent orange jackets so that they wouldn't get hit by a train by mistake. They seemed bloody sure of themselves that there weren't any snipers around.

Too bad he hadn't a rifle with him. Momentarily, Mike Carney's fingers twitched. People that cock-sure of themselves deserved to be taken down a peg or two; to be picked off like pigeons in the spring mating season – and paying just about as much attention to the possible dangers around them. Did the fools seriously imagine that anyone was going to clamber up on the bridge and drop something on the Lord Mayor's coach as he passed under it?

Just like the police. Either no imagination at all, or else too much. But none of them were clever enough to match him. He'd give them half a mile for a headstart and still leave them standing.

But they knew something was wrong. Mike Carney frowned down on Kitty. How much else did they know?

He hadn't expected them to twig on to that much this soon. The brat's mother, probably. Women weren't to be depended on – any of them. Probably she'd sneaked away from her job early and gone looking for the kid. And when she couldn't find

her, what then? Had she talked to the landlady?
The police? Had his room been searched? What had
they found? Had he tidied things away well enough?
He'd been in a tearing hurry towards the last.
Or had he – ?

'Da – ' Kitty tugged at his hand. 'Da – '

'Shut up!' He just stopped himself hitting her.
'Can't you see I'm thinking?'

'But Da – ' she would not be hushed. 'Da, it's
raining.'

'Do you think I haven't seen that?' A soft glow of
satisfaction spread through him as he watched them
all scurrying for the shelter of the railway bridge.
They'd be packed in there like sardines. And just
wait until the tin was ripped open!

'Da – ' She tugged again. 'I'm getting wet. My
mother doesn't like me to get wet. I'll catch cold.'

'Don't worry about that,' he said. 'She won't be
mad at you. She won't mind at all.'

'But Da – ' she was still dubious. 'I don't *want* to
get all wet. I don't like it.'

'All right, all right.' Grudgingly, as though it
were her idea, as though he were indulging her
against his better judgement, he gave in. 'Hurry
along then and we'll get under the bridge. I suppose
we can see as well there as anywhere.'

'Oh, *thank* you, Da.' She accepted his capitula-
tion as her due. 'We can see all right from there.
I *know* we can!' She gave a little skip as she tugged
him towards her goal.

'Don't dawdle, Timothy . . . Come along,
Geraldine!' With a half-smile of perplexed semi-
recognition, the woman from Paternoster Square
herded her children past them, also hurrying for the

shelter of the railway bridge.

Mike Carney nodded pleasantly to her as she passed, mentally racking up three more victims. That was more like it. Another serpent and her hissing little vipers to be wiped out. So they ought to perish, all of them. Little snakes grew up into big snakes. Sometimes into great grasping boa constrictors throttling the life out of –

'*Da!*'

Couldn't bear being ignored for one moment, the little Madam! It would be a service to the world to rid it of that one!

'*Da!*'

'All right, what is it?' He tried to smile.

'That was the lady who took me to the loo. I like her. Can't we go and talk to her?'

'No, we can't!' he snapped.

'I want to!' Her lower lip jutted out threateningly. 'I *want* to.'

'She's a busy lady.' Quickly, he tried to soften it, to evade the threatened scene. 'She's got her own kids to cope with. She can't be bothered with the likes of you today.'

'Their Daddy is in the parade,' Kitty said. 'He's riding in a big carriage.'

'Is he, by God?' Suddenly interested, Carney lengthened his stride. 'Which one, did the lady tell you that?'

'I don't know. The little girl told me.' Kitty stumbled and protested, 'Da – you're going too fast again.'

'Sorry.' He slowed only because he had seen the stumble. If she should fall now it would be the end of all his plans. He had to be careful of her for just this little while longer. 'Just watch where you're going.'

They were coming into the thick of the crowd again. Not even the rain was thinning it out much. People had come too far to give up now, just as the main part of the procession was reaching them. They were prepared to hold out for just a bit longer.

But Kitty was holding back, dragging on him. He looked down and saw the stormclouds gathering on her face.

'Come along,' he cajoled. 'You want to catch up with your friends, don't you?'

But her mood had changed again. 'No,' she said stubbornly.

'Aaah, of course you do,' he said. He wanted to learn more about them now, find out who they were, keep close to them, make sure they didn't escape. If they had someone riding in a carriage, they should not escape, they ought to be in the target area. 'Just a little bit faster and we'll catch them up.'

'I'm tired.' She slanted a semi-flirtatious glance upwards at him. 'Carry me again.'

'We're nearly there.' He tried to keep his emotions out of his face. 'Just down there is where we're going. You don't need to be carried that little way.'

She halted. 'I'm tired,' she said stubbornly.

'You're a big girl now.' He was equally stubborn, knowing that if she got up on his shoulders again she would be impossible to dislodge. She would insist on watching the proceedings from up there – and how could he get the lunch box away from her? 'You don't want to be carried like a little baby.'

'I'm tired.' She refused to move. It was a flat-out clash of wills. 'I'm too tired. I want to go home.'

Somehow she had sensed that was a winning card to play.

'A big girl like you.' He pulled at her hand. 'Aren't you ashamed? Come on now, behave yourself.'

'No!' Was she going to cry? Would it make any difference if she did? A lot of the kids had cried, or would cry, at some point during the day. The excitement was too much for them.

But it was a danger signal. She was definitely fretful – and fretful children were unpredictable. He was thankful he had not planned his coup for later in the day. She'd never have stuck it out that long – maybe he was lucky she had lasted this long. He didn't know enough about kids, that was the problem. If he'd known half what he knew about them now – and about Kitty in particular – he'd never have bothered with her. He'd have thought of some other way.

Kids had tantrums, he knew that. Suddenly, his blood chilled.

'All right.' He picked her up as roughly as he dared and started forward.

'Up higher,' she protested. 'I want to ride on your shoulders.'

'This is as high as you're going,' he said grimly. She wouldn't have got this much of a concession if it weren't for the thought he had suddenly had. 'And I'm putting you down when we get to the bridge.'

With an effort, he became placatory once more. 'You'll want to get out in front of the crowd. If we can stand you at the curb, you'll see a lot better.'

'Oooh.' Perhaps she had reservations. If so, she

obviously decided that a concession of her own was necessary – at least for the moment. 'All right,' she said.

Carney strode ahead grimly. He had forestalled the threatened tantrum, but he still felt weak at the thought of it.

When kids had tantrums, they threw things.

CHAPTER XXVI

In the open spaces around St Paul's, Lutterworth felt there was a certain safety. Lower Ludgate Hill had an open bombsite, now a car park, on one side of the approach to the railway bridge, and he could see the policemen patrolling on top of the bridge itself. So far, so good. Then Ludgate Circus, a no-man's-land of more wide open space, probably the last open island of safety before the danger ahead.

Safety ended on the other side of Ludgate Circus, where the narrow corridor of Fleet Street lurked between looming buildings filled with people watching the parade. Every window, from first floor to the topmost level, would be crammed with spectators. And Carney might be in any of those windows, waiting to drop it on them.

But Lutterworth had another big worry now. Clover the Clown had cracked up once and might again at any instant. His pennyfarthing was swerving erratically back and forth across the road, and he kept muttering to himself. Words that made no sense when you got close enough to hear. Why should he be worrying about Connecticut at a time like this?

However, the clown was back in the centre of the road at the moment and smiling, so far as one could determine beneath the heavy mask of greasepaint. So far, so good. But how much farther?

If Clover could keep going until they reached the

Royal Courts of Justice – if they got that far –
then it might be possible to get some tranquillizers
into him to keep him going for the rest of the way.

In fact, once they got to the Royal Courts of
Justice, things would be easier all around. While the
Lord Mayor and his entourage were lunching
within, the police would have another hour in
hand in which to intensify the search over a narrower
field. Once they got to the Royal Courts of Justice,
their chances would automatically improve, the
odds lengthening in their favour. Once they got to
the Royal Courts of Justice . . .

If they got to the Royal Courts of Justice . . .

Meanwhile, every few feet they advanced freed
policemen who had been guarding that territory
to leave their posts and move ahead to establish
fresh observation posts.

Even now there was unobtrusive movement on
the pavement, a quietly purposeful flow of people
forming the background to the eddy of restless
members of the crowd.

Some of them, no doubt, were cutting down side
streets, forging their way towards the lurking
dangers of Fleet Street; rather, the hovering
dangers. All those windows. Lutterworth felt his
stomach contract.

It had been said that if someone was determined
to kill a prominent personality, there was a good
chance that he would succeed. And it was true.
A new grim knowledge was abroad in the world.
Political assassination had become a present reality,
rather than a distant event in history books dotted
with names like Ford's Theatre and Sarajevo.

If someone was determined enough, he could

succeed. Despite bodyguards, despite police protection, despite the best efforts of modern science and technology to prevent it.

The helicopter clattered uselessly overhead. In this case, an instrument of possible retribution, rather than rescue. Good only for the chase which might ensue, but powerless to intercept a bomb dropped from a window or hurled out of the crowd.

For that matter, how much better would any of them be? (How much better had the guards surrounding the Kennedy brothers been?) A guard – any guard – was only as good as the luck which placed him in the right spot at the right moment. And, more importantly, with enough moments in hand to realize the situation and move to do something about it.

Clover began wavering again. The pennyfarthing wobbled and threatened to swoop towards the children at the curb. Clover's face was brooding and intent, his eyes gazed into the distance unseeingly, while the first heavy droplets of rain splattered into his face and rolled down his cheeks like tears.

Lutterworth moved forward, crowding Clover back into the centre of the road. Clover looked down at him mournfully.

'Pull yourself together!' Lutterworth snapped, his irritation rising. He had enough to do without having to worry about the clown as well. 'You're not helping, you know!'

Clover nodded, still mournful. He knew. He was no help at all. He turned away, pedalling slowly, remembering to wave to the children along the way. It was all he could do. He was meant to be entertaining them, making them laugh. When it might be the last thing they ever laughed at.

The pennyfarthing abruptly halted and bucked as though it were trying to dislodge him. Clover fought it frantically, sliding up and down in his seat as it bucked, then chased itself in circles. This was what the kids expected. They shrieked their approval.

As he wrestled with the machine, one of his fellow clowns ran up to help him and obligingly let himself be chased by the pennyfarthing. They skittered about wildly for a minute, then Lutterworth placed his hand on the big wheel.

'That's enough,' he said. 'You're holding up the parade. Let's keep moving.'

Clover nodded and pantomimed gratitude. The children cheered his rescuer. He became aware of the excessive wetness on his cheeks, the blurring of his vision. He brushed away the rain – and the tears.

Inexorably, the parade moved on.

'What's the hold-up?' Sir Guy Carraway leaned out of the coach window and queried Barney.

'Something ahead – ' Barney, who had the advantage of mobility, swung away from the coach for a better view. The children along both sides of the street were trying to push forward to watch something happening just ahead. They were laughing. Some policemen were straining to hold them back before they burst into the street. The police were laughing, too.

Barney darted forward – first to one side of the street, then the other – releasing a compartment of blackbird vouchers on each side, giving them an extra impetus that sent them fluttering over the heads of the children immediately in front.

That gave the kiddies something else to think about. They scrambled for the vouchers, easing the pressure on the police. It also gave Barney a clearer field to view the situation ahead.

'It's all right, Lucky.' He reported back to Guy. 'It's only the clown – ' he shrugged wryly – 'clowning.'

'Good.' Guy leaned back in his seat. 'That's what we want him to do. Business as usual.'

'In his case,' Barney corrected, 'The Show Must Go On.' He thought momentarily. 'In all our cases – today.'

'The Lord Mayor's Show – ' It came out on a sigh, and Guy straightened up. *Keep smiling, keep waving.* 'Let's hope this isn't the one that makes the history books.'

'It's raining, Lucky.' Barney tried to cheer him. 'Just a little bit harder and a lot of people are going to get discouraged and go home. Maybe even your mad bomber. You know those types – erratic. Doesn't take much to start 'em off, and doesd't take much to turn 'em off. A good old downpour could do it. With your luck – look, it's coming down harder already.'

'Not hard enough.' Guy turned away, towards the other window. *Smile-and-wave, smile-and-wave.*

'Let's face it, Barney.' His voice floated back to Barney with a curiously hollow note in it. 'My luck may have run out.'

As the rain began splattering down, Elaine sprinted

the remaining few yards to the shelter of the railway bridge. At least, she tried to sprint. As much as one could with two children in tow, and in competition with twenty or thirty other people with the same idea, all heading in the same direction.

'Don't *dawdle*, Geraldine!' She tugged at the child's hand. Geraldine had tried to halt to watch a bit of by-play the clowns were indulging in.

'Don't *dawdle*, Timothy!' Geraldine imitated her mother's tone, giving her brother a push as he hesitated to see what she was looking at. Then her attention was caught by a waving hand farther up the hill. 'Look, mother – there's that little girl again.'

'Yes, yes,' Elaine said abstractedly. She had spotted a familiar figure herself. 'Isn't that Auntie Jean? There ahead, with Little Jean?'

'It *is*!' Geraldine took the lead now, pulling the others along. 'Auntie Jean – ' she called. 'Auntie Jean – wait for us!'

On the second shout, the woman ahead turned, laughed and waved. She pointed towards the railway bridge and signalled that she would meet them under it.

Elaine waved agreement, and concentrated on negotiating the narrowing pathway left by the crowds. Absently, she noted the police guards patrolling the top of the bridge, highly visible in their fluorescent orange jackets. Were they there to stop the trains until the parade had passed? But that was silly. The street traffic had been stopped, but they wouldn't need to stop overhead trains. Shrugging mentally, she forgot the stray thought.

They crossed Seacoal Lane, the final side street before the bridge, not noticing a pair of ambulances waiting in the side turning.

The rain was heavier, but there was already a faint brightening of the sky on the horizon. (*Let it stop raining. This is Guy's big day. He's done so much,* she bargained fiercely with the Lord. *He'll do so much more. He deserves to have everything perfect today. Let it stop raining.*)

'I *thought* we'd meet up somewhere along the way!' Jean hailed them, laughing. They herded together and the crowd shifted slightly to allow them room under the bridge.

'We were bound to,' Elaine agreed.

'How many times have you seen Daddy?' the children compared notes. 'This is our third time. When are we going to eat?'

'I'm not really hungry,' Elaine said. 'Too excited, perhaps.'

'Neither am I,' Jean said. 'But I suppose we ought to feed the children. There's a place around the corner in Farringdon Street where we can get coffee and all sorts of fancy doughnuts. That ought to keep them happy.'

'I know the place,' Elaine nodded. 'It will be just right. There'll probably be an enormous queue, though. I should think half the people here have it marked out in the back of their minds for a snack.'

'It shouldn't be too bad if we can get there before the crowd breaks up.' Jean looked around with an assessing eye. 'If we move to the far side of the bridge and make a break for it as soon as our darlings have gone past, we ought to beat the worst of the rush.'

'That's a good idea.' Elaine gently urged the children forward. 'I must admit a cup of coffee would be very welcome right now – even if everyone

THE LORD MAYOR OF DEATH   173

else in the City *does* want one at the same time.'

'This ought to be far enough.' Jean halted them
just under the bridge on the Ludgate Circus side.
'We're still protected from the rain here, but we're
close enough to make a dash for it as soon as the
coach has gone by.'

'Yes.' Elaine looked up Ludgate Hill, watching
the slow approach of the only part of the parade
she cared about. She turned back to Jean. 'Isn't
it strange – ?'

'Who would have dreamed – ?' Jean began at the
same time.

They laughed spontaneously, knowing they were
sharing the same thoughts, the same memories.

'Oh, isn't this fun!' Elaine cried. 'Isn't life
wonderful?'

CHAPTER XXVII

'Oh, my God, it's a nightmare,' Maureen moaned. 'A nightmare. Why can't I wake up?'

'It's all right,' Donovan said falsely. 'Just don't worry. It's going to be all right.'

'All right!' She sagged against him. His arm was around her shoulders, had been around her shoulders for some time, supporting her. Now he was practically carrying her.

'Sure, all right.' He exchanged a desperate glance with Hilary. People were looking at them curiously, wondering why a woman in such a condition was out on a day like this.

'Maybe if we stopped by one of the ambulances,' he muttered to Hilary. 'They might be able to give us something to help her. Keep her going.'

'I'll keep going.' Maureen heard the last bit. 'I'll keep going.' She raised her head from his shoulder, trying to fight free of his arm. 'You needn't worry about me. It's Kitty we've got to worry about. Kitty!'

'That's right,' he soothed. 'That's right.' He tightened his arm, keeping her imprisoned. 'Don't worry, we'll find her.'

'Perhaps if we turn down here – ' Hilary signalled to Donovan. There were two ambulances standing a little way down Ave Maria Lane. If they could get her to one of them –

'No! No!' Suddenly aware of the benevolent plot against her, Maureen began struggling to get away from them.

'All right, take it easy.' Donovan tightened his grip, restraining her. 'We won't do anything you don't want us to do.'

'I want Kitty,' she choked. 'My little Kitty. Where is she?' She looked around wildly. 'Where *is* she?'

Donovan and Hilary looked at each other helplessly. There were children everywhere – and not one of them was the right one. So far as they could see. The trouble was that all the children were beginning to look alike. There were multitudes of them, each indistinguishable from the others.

Nor was the situation helped by the fact that all the children were facing the other way. The best way to try to spot a particular child would be to march in the parade itself. The children were all intent on that. From the narrow passageway left at the rear of the pavement, only the backs of heads could be seen.

It was easier to spot her fellow constables – uniformed or not. They were the ones who were watching the crowd rather than the parade. Their eyes were alert, their faces taut; people who knew what was at stake. They were bringing the best they had to bear upon the situation. But it was going to take more than just their best. It was going to take luck.

The luck of Lucky Guy.

Sir Guy Carraway. He was nearly opposite them now, the three pairs of handsome prancing Shire horses effortlessly pulling the gilded coach.

And, alone in the coach, Sir Guy Carraway sat smiling and waving as though he hadn't a care in the world. As though he were not perfectly aware

176 THE LORD MAYOR OF DEATH

that he was a terrorist's target for today. Lucky
Guy.

Hilary didn't know about his luck, but no one
could fault the man's guts.

They were at Old Bailey now. The Old Bailey itself
stood farther along the turning. Hilary lifted her
eyes with foreboding to look at the blindfolded
statue of Justice standing atop it. There had already
been one bomb attack on the Old Bailey –

The explosion sounded directly behind them.
Both Hilary and Maureen screamed. Donovan
paled. They swung round as one unit.

'Blood!' Maureen gasped, pointing downward.
'Oh, God – blood!'

They looked at the dark crimson splash at her
feet, afraid to look beyond it for the devastation.
Then Donovan gave a mirthless laugh and stooped
and picked it up.

'It's all right,' he said. 'It's just one of the
Remembrance Day poppies come off its stem. It
isn't blood.'

Of course. The poppy sellers were everywhere.
They had been accosted by several, but had been
too intent on their own mission to stop long enough
to buy a poppy. Most of the crowd wore one.

'But the noise,' Maureen said. 'The explosion.'

'Only a balloon bursting.' Donovan waved
towards a disconsolate child looking forlornly at a
few bright red tatters of rubber hanging at the end
of a stick. 'It just sounded loud to us because we
were expecting – ' He broke off quickly.

'I mean,' he amended, 'because we were so close,
and it was so, so sudden, like.'

'Oh, throw it away!' He had forgotten he was

still holding the crimson patch until Maureen cried out. 'It's horrible – nightmarish!'

'Sorry – ' He let it flutter back to the ground. 'I wasn't thinking . . .'

But they were all thinking. Too much. At the periphery of her vision, Hilary was still aware of the red shreds of balloon being waved by the child. She looked down at the crimson on the pavement. Even when one knew what it was, it still looked like a splash of blood. Perhaps the next red they saw *woulde* be –

'Come,' she said abruptly. 'Let's go on.'

He was seeing red, Mike Carney thought. This was what the expression meant. As though a thin film of blood had spread across his retina and he was viewing the world through that. The crowd had faded out into the monochrome pinkish-sepia of an old photograph. The only bits of colour were the Remembrance Day poppies some of them were wearing. The poppies blossomed on bosoms and in buttonholes like the exit wounds of bullets.

It wouldn't be long now.

'Here we are.' He slid Kitty to the ground despite her protests.

'No – ' she tried to cling to him. 'No, I want to see everything.'

'You can see better down here,' he said firmly. He wanted that lunch box within easy snatching distance. Time was getting very short. The Lord Mayor's coach was in clear sight, proceeding majestically down Ludgate Hill.

'Look – ' Kitty was momentarily distracted. 'There's that lady and the children again. Over there!' She pointed to the opposite end of the bridge.

'Just never you mind them!' He took a firm grip on her hand. 'Let them be. They're nothing to us.'

'But – '

'Get along to the front there.' He nudged her forward. 'You want to see, don't you?'

'Yes.' She began to co-operate, twisting her way through the crowd, taking advantage of every slight opening in their ranks.

'That's the girl,' he encouraged her. 'That's the way to do it.'

Intent on getting to the front, she paid no attention to him. In fact, she seemed to forget he was there. He kept hold of her hand.

'Just let the kiddie through, will you?' He spoke to some adults blocking their path. 'She's never seen the parade before.' He smiled ingratiatingly. 'It's her first time.'

They moved aside and made no remarks about the way he was edging along behind the child, although he'd been half-expecting some rudeness and was prepared to cite her age and size as the excuse for not letting go of her. But no one seemed to mind. They were a good-natured crowd. Maybe they'd never again be quite so forbearing with a stranger. But then, maybe they'd never get the chance again. Blast did funny things.

'There you are, lovey.' They had reached the front and he risked the endearment, knowing that she was oblivious of him. 'I promised you we'd see Clover and the Lord Mayor again, didn't I?'

The parade had halted momentarily to allow a bit of by-play between the clowns. They were wheeling about all over the place, the kids laughing

their heads off at them. Fools! All of them! Fools!
They deserved what they were going to get. He
only wished he could take care of more of them. That
the clowns could be included in the explosion, but
they were likely to be out of the way by then.

After what seemed an interminable time to him,
they began moving forward again. He tensed,
trying to judge their pace, which was still erratic.
Was it time to prepare?

He looked down at Kitty. She was completely
engrossed in the panorama spreading itself out
before them. The little red lunch box in her hand
seemed redder than anything else around, as though
it were glowing with an inner light of its own.

Casually, he dropped one hand on to Kitty's
shoulder, scarcely feeling it shift irritably under the
weight of his hand.

That was better, so much nearer his goal now.
Just a quick dip of the hand, a tug at the lunch
box, and it would be in his hand for the hurling.
And his goal was rolling nearer by the moment.

He hadn't thought clearly beyond that. Beyond
that, it didn't seem to matter. He'd start to run as
he hurled it – He'd planned that much – knocking
the unsuspecting bystanders out of his way. He had
a sporting chance of getting free, having taken
everyone by surprise. Maybe he'd drag Kitty a
bit of the way with him, having first given her a good
clip across the ear to start her crying and further
confuse the situation. Then he could hurl her in the
path of any possible pursuers. The flaw in that was
that he'd be taking her out of the range of the bomb
and, after the day she had given him, she didn't
deserve that much of a break. No, leave her where

she was – right in front.

The clowns were nearly opposite, the Lord Mayor's coach immediately in their wake.

Mike Carney felt a wave of elation sweep over him. He'd done it. He'd brought it off. He was here – lying in wait with the bomb that was going to make world headlines, put his name into the history books – and no one suspected him. He'd been more clever than any of them. He'd done it – or as good as. He was the stuff heroes were made of. Nothing could stop him now.

Kitty wriggled her shoulder impatiently in another effort to dislodge the oppressive hand. She hadn't been positive before, her emotions had wavered between two decisions, but now she knew.

She didn't like Uncle Mike. Or Da. Or whatever she ought to be calling him. Under any name, she didn't like him. As soon as she got home again, she was going to shut herself in Mummy's room and never open the door again if Uncle Mike were standing outside. She shouldn't have today. Mummy had told her never to. No matter who was standing outside the door calling so coaxingly.

Of course, she was glad to be seeing the parade. She wouldn't want to change that. But it would have been nicer to be here with Mummy instead of Uncle Mike. There was something uncomfortable about being with him, something that had grown more uncomfortable as the day wore on.

Kitty wriggled her shoulder again. Once more, without success. No, she definitely didn't like Uncle Mike. Not even a little bit.

She glanced up at him. He was looking very

strange. His eyes had a funny look in them and he was watching the slow advance of the clowns as though he weren't really seeing them at all.

She decided not to say anything to him. Except for that heavy hand on her shoulder, he seemed to have forgotten her presence. She decided that she didn't really want to remind him of it. She wished she were not utterly dependent on him to get her home safely.

Laughter from the crowd brought her attention back to the centre of the road. Clover was pedalling along furiously, waving to all the children along the way. They were waving back.

She liked Clover. She wanted to wave, but Uncle Mike had a hurting grip on one hand, and her lunch box was in the other. She lifted the hand, lunch box and all, and waved enthusiastically.

'What do you think you're doing?' Uncle Mike's sudden shout startled her. 'Stop jarring your lunch box like that! Do you want to ruin everything?'

Kitty shrank away from him, instinctively looking to those around her for protection. But no one was paying any attention. Everyone was watching the parade.

'Give me that!' He lunged for the lunch box, but met unexpected resistance.

'No!' Kitty clung to it desperately. He had given it to her, he could not take it away again. She hadn't done anything wrong. Nothing to be punished like that for.

'Let me have it!' He spoke between clenched teeth, keeping his voice low.

'No! It's mine! You said it was!'

All he needed, to become involved in a tug o' war

with a stubborn little brat. Mike Carney cast a
furtive look over the surrounding crowd, wondering
if anyone would notice if he knocked her senseless.

But there was always someone watching. He
encountered a pair of amused eyes, familiar eyes.
The woman who'd taken Kitty down to the Ladies
in Paternoster Square. Nosy, interfering bitch!

He tried to smile, but the expression on his face
must have been subtly wrong. Already the expression
in the woman's eyes was changing. The amusement had given way to uneasiness and, behind the
uneasiness, was the beginning of suspicion.

'Give it me,' he said urgently. 'I'll give it back
to you in a minute.' The clowns were nearly past,
the Lord Mayor's coach would be upon them. 'I
– I just want to – to check something.'

'No!' All the pent-up frustrations of the day burst
forth. 'I don't like you, Uncle Mike. I don't like
you at all!'

'I don't care what you like!' He let go of her hand
to use both hands to wrench the lunch box away
from her. 'Give me that!'

'I won't!' He was bigger and stronger than she
was, and he was winning. Feeling the lunch box
begin to slip from her grasp, she lashed out with her
foot. The metal-tipped toe caught him sharply on
the ankle bone.

The world went redder than ever. For a moment,
there was only the excruciating pain. Then, as it
faded, he realized that he'd let go of her. With
blood in his eye, he started for her, hands outstretched, momentarily more concerned to get them
around her throat than on the lunch box.

Kitty backed away warily. She'd gone too far.

Grown-ups expected that they could go as far as they liked, but when you fought back, they got mad. It wasn't fair. He was going to hit her! She looked around wildly, for help, for protection.

Clover! He was directly opposite her, nearer than anybody else – except Uncle Mike, who was cutting her off from the crowd.

Clover would help. He was her friend, she'd seen him on television. Clover *liked* to help children. And Clover was sad, Clover was crying, brushing away tears. Perhaps she could help Clover, too. She'd give anything to cheer him up.

She'd give – But all she had to give was her new lunch box. Would he like it? Was it good enough for him?

'Come here to me, Kitty.' The frightening voice sounded from behind her. 'Come give me that!' It convinced her that the lunch box was a treasure worth bestowing.

'I won't give it to you!' She whirled on him, still backing away. 'I'll – I'll give it to Clover!' She turned and darted out into the street.

Lutterworth saw the child coming. Just one more anonymous child in the regulation uniform and little yellow sou'wester. At first, he thought she was trying to dash across the street before the rest of the parade came along.

But she stopped at Clover's pennyfarthing, looking up at him earnestly, telling him something.

Lutterworth moved closer.

Then he became aware of the man at the edge of the crowd watching the child intently, starting forward and moving back indecisively. Surely, any father had a right to be concerned if his daughter had darted into the street to hold up the progress of a parade.

But any ordinary father might have already rushed forward apologetically to pull her back to the pavement. Or was this one just extraordinarily diffident?

Even as he wondered, Lutterworth saw the man square his shoulders and begin to move forward determinedly.

The child reached up to Clover, offering him her little lunch box. Clover still seemed disoriented and confused. With the underlying crisis to worry about, he had probably forgotten the usual attitude of his fans and their little offerings to him.

'Take it, Clover,' the child's clear voice urged. 'It's for you. So you can stop feeling sad.'

She stood on tiptoe, holding the lunch box up to him.

As Clover gathered himself together and reached down to accept it, she tilted her head even farther back in order to see him more clearly. The brim of her little yellow sou'wester hit against the collar of her coat and the sou'wester slowly slid away from her head and slipped to the ground.

The shining red curls tumbled free.

'Kitty!' A woman's voice screamed from the crowd. 'Kitty!'

CHAPTER XXVIII

Clover leaned down and graciously accepted the lunch box since the sweet little girl so obviously wished him to. He smiled down vaguely, still lost in his private hell, unable to hear clearly what she was trying to tell him. There was too much competition from the band immediately in front and from the crowd. Clover noted anxiously that more of the kiddies were getting restless, squirming against restraining hands. If he didn't get rid of this one quickly and start moving again, they would rush out and mob him. He didn't mind that happening when he was on foot, but when he was perched high on the pennyfarthing, all those crowding, pushing children were a frightening prospect. Moments like this reminded him how vulnerable he was. The pennyfarthing was a great gimmick but, basically, it was as tricky as being on stilts.

Apparently satisfied, the child turned and stooped to pick up her fallen sou'wester.

'Kitty! Kitty!' Two women, one of them with hair as red as the child's own, broke free of the crowd and swooped towards her. Behind them, a man followed more slowly, gazing thoughtfully back at the crowd, as though searching for someone.

Lutterworth started running forward, shouting something incomprehensible. Clover gradually began to realize what it all might mean – what he could be holding in his hands. He was suddenly thankful for the thick white cotton clown gloves he

wore. Inside them, his hands had produced a
sudden sweat which otherwise might have let the
red lunch box slip from them.

'Back!' Lutterworth shouted. 'Back – !' He waved
his arms wildly, directing traffic which consisted
only of a lone pennyfarthing driven by a frightened
clown whose reactions were in danger of being
paralysed by sheer terror.

'Back!' Lutterworth shouted. 'Take it to the
police car following the Lord Mayor's coach.
Quickly! And – for God's sake – don't drop it,
man!'

Don't drop it. The nightmare was in his hands
now. Clover ponderously wheeled the pennyfarthing about, trying not to think too clearly about
what was at stake. The length of Ludgate Hill
loomed before him – a steeper incline than it had
seemed on the way down.

He began fighting with the pedals, pushing his
way upwards. He wasn't accustomed to anything
like this – nor was the pennyfarthing. They were
both just slightly out of date for anything so ener-
getic. It was like trying to fight his way through a sea
of congealing glue.

Then, out of the corner of his eye, he became
aware of the worst menace of all. He fought with the
intractable pedals, but they fought back and the
distance he gained was minimal. He saw the amazed
face of Sir Guy Carraway as he watched the utterly
unscheduled and unexpected approach of the pennyfarthing, but he could do nothing about that.

Suddenly, full awareness flooded through him.
He knew exactly what was at stake: all those children. Their lives were literally in his hands. He had

to deliver the – Yes, the *bomb*, into the hands of the police in the patrol car behind the Lord Mayor's coach, so that they could wheel out of the parade, away from the crowds, and take it to a piece of open land to await the arrival of the bomb disposal squad.

He *had* to.

Clover concentrated on fighting the penny-farthing up Ludgate Hill, trying to ignore the madman who was charging at him out of the crowd.

Mike Carney stood frozen in an unbelieving daze as he watched everything coming apart right in front of his eyes.

How had she got away from him? A dull ache in his ankle was only partially responsible. He should have held on to her, no matter what.

Now there she was, brazen as brass, out there talking sixteen to the dozen to that fool clown and God alone knowing what she was saying to him.

Giving him the lunch box! Oh, the betrayal!

'Kitty! Kitty!' And there was the O'Fahey woman – her stupid mother! What was she doing here? How had she found out so soon? But here she was – and rushing forward out of the crowd to claim her brat. Her little bastard!

It was over. Finished. They had – no, not outsmarted him. But the luck – that was it, the luck – was running against him.

Old Lucky Guy. Sir Guy Carraway, Lord Mayor of London. And that was it. He should never have gone up against Lucky Guy. St Patrick and all the leprechauns of the Emerald Isle could not prevail against him. Not prevail against real luck. That was

what you needed in this life: luck above everything
else.

But it wasn't done yet. Not quite yet. (The
world was brighter – redder – than ever. He saw
everything clearly now, although still tinged by
that crimson haze.) There was one chance left.

Maybe he'd not get the Lord Mayor, but he'd
get that interfering clown – and Kitty. He hoped to
God he'd get that rotten little brat!

He lowered his head and charged straight at the
pennyfarthing. Just knock that over and it would be
as good as hurling the bomb. The effect would be
the same.

Clover saw him coming. He swerved the pennyfarthing aside, pedalling frantically. He saw Lutterworth race forward to try to block the madman,
and saw Lutterworth slip and fall.

The rain was ending now, but the long slope of
Ludgate Hill shone with the greasy iridescence of oil
slicks made twice as slippery by the downpour.
Clover felt the wheels of the pennyfarthing begin
to slide and lose traction. He eased it into a lower
gear, aware that the man behind him was running
faster than he could propel the machine. Even
providing the pennyfarthing could keep traction
on the hill and not start sliding backwards, back
to the foot of the hill and all those children.

Hilary felt her initial fury growing into a towering
rage that threatened to bring tears to her eyes.

As she had tried to approach Mike Carney to
arrest him, that hulking oaf of a clown had shoul-
dered her aside, knocking her out of the way and
running after Carney himself.

It served him right! She glowed with momentary satisfaction to see him slip and fall, but then she remembered what was at stake. And Mike Carney was still charging straight at Clover, defenceless atop his pennyfarthing.

Pat Donovan, after making sure that Kitty and Maureen were safely reunited, moved forward grimly to join in the chase. He owed that one a lump or two for all the misery he had caused. And was still trying to cause.

The other clowns were heading for Carney as well. The purposefulness of their movements brought it home to Donovan that they were something more than they seemed. He caught the eye of one of them and, obeying the short sharp jerk of his head, fell into line in the gap left by the clown who had fallen.

Lutterworth picked himself up quickly, not wasting any breath on curses, and hurtled after Carney again. It had seemed to take for ever, but Carney was not that much ahead of him. The hill was steep and slippery for both of them.

Nor was Clover gaining much ground. Still pedalling for all he was worth, he was not propelling the pennyfarthing nearly fast enough to keep away from Mike Carney. It was going to be up to the foot troops.

The children along the way whooped with delight at this extra attraction. They cheered on Clover and the clowns. Some of them even decided to cheer for Mike Carney. Their laughter would become part of future nightmares – if Carney wasn't stopped in time.

His breath sobbing in his throat, Mike Carney tried to weave in unison with the pennyfarthing. The laughter of the children maddened him. The clown was playing with him, like a matador playing a bull. Letting him think he was going to hit the pennyfarthing each time he charged, then swerving aside at the last second. And each time gaining a bit of an advance up the hill to the police cars following in the wake of the parade.

But the police stationed along the parade route were beginning to realize that this wasn't part of the Show. Some of them were quietly making their way to places that would block off any possible way of escape for him.

But there was no thought of escape in his mind now. There was only one wild determination. They were all going to go together. And . . . N O W !

The brakes locked suddenly on the pennyfarthing. It came to a standstill. Clover stamped frantically on the pedals, but the machine would not move forward. It was a genuine antique and, under so much sudden pressure, had resorted to temperament. He was a sitting target now. He could only sit and watch Carney and Lutterworth racing towards him on a collision course.

Lutterworth took a deep breath and the only chance that was open to him now. He hurled himself forward in a flying tackle.

Mike Carney felt himself falling. He stretched out as he went down, trying to reach the pennyfarthing and Clover and bring them down with him, but his fingers grazed the street just short of the pennyfarthing which had abruptly begun to move again.

Carney lashed out with his feet and had the satisfaction of feeling his boot encounter a face. But his captor did not let go. Carney heard running footsteps all around him and saw the ring of feet surrounding him. He rolled over on his back, staring up blankly at the brightening sky and cursed them and the world in both English and Gaelic.

Suddenly, the brakes unjammed themselves, the machine bucked briefly, then moved forward majestically. Clover kept it moving automatically, so limp with relief that he was nearly an automaton himself. The madman had been brought down, the child was safe, and the bomb was still in his hands, unexploded.

All the children, all his precious little ones, were safe.

The police car behind the Lord Mayor's coach swung open its doors. One of the policemen got out and came over to meet Clover, holding up his arms.

'Right, mate,' he said. 'Lower it gently. *Very* gently.'

Lutterworth straightened slowly as they marched Mike Carney away and looked up Ludgate Hill. The Lord Mayor was out of his coach and shaking Clover's hand. Behind them, the klaxon of the police car began to sound as the car peeled away from the procession and sped for open ground to await the bomb disposal squad. The rain had stopped and it even looked as though the sun might be trying to shine through the remaining clouds.

He and his fellow clowns, in order to keep the crowd unsuspecting, would escort Clover as far as

the Royal Courts of Justice and slip away when the
Lord Mayor and his entourage went in to lunch.

An angry tug at his arm brought his attention
down to a pair of blazing eyes.

'Did you hear me?' Hilary asked sharply. 'I said
you're under arrest.'

'Arrest? What for?'

'Obstructing an officer. You kept pushing me out
of the way every time I tried to get near enough
to the bomber to apprehend him.' She opened her
shoulder bag and a warrant card flashed in her
hand. 'I'm taking you into custody.'

Lutterworth began to grin broadly. Suddenly it
all began to seem true. The nightmare was over.
They'd won – all of them. The danger was past,
the future stretched before them again.

'Lovely, darling,' he said. His own warrant card
winked back at her. 'Meet me at the Royal Courts
of Justice in about half an hour and we've got a
date!'

'Uncle Pat,' Kitty said fretfully. 'I don't like Uncle
Mike. I don't like him at all.'

'Never mind, he's gone now,' Donovan said
abstractedly. He'd replaced his arm around Maureen
and she hadn't seemed to mind. Perhaps she'd grown
used to having it there. He decided to chance his
other arm.

'How about me? You like me all right, don't
you?' He watched Maureen, who was very carefully
not looking at him, and they both waited for
Kitty's answer.

'Ye . . . es,' Kitty said slowly, still seeming
bothered. 'But I don't like that Uncle Mike. I

don't want to see him again.'

'That's all right,' Donovan said, feeling Maureen relax against him. 'You won't have to see him ever again.'

'Not ever?' Kitty looked hopeful. 'But he lives back at our house.'

'Not any more,' Donovan said.